Wish

www.chellebliss.com

CHELLE BLISS

USA TODAY BESTSELLING AUTHOR

WISH COPYRIGHT © 2025

No part of this book may be reproduced or transmitted in any form, including electronic or mechanical, without written permission from the publisher, except in the case of brief quotations embodied in critical articles or reviews. This is a work of fiction. Names, characters, businesses, places, events, and incidents are either the products of the author's imagination or used in a fictitious manner. Any resemblance to actual persons, living or dead, or actual events is purely coincidental. This book may not be resold or given away to other people. If you would like to share this book with another person, please purchase an additional copy for each person you share it with. If you are reading this book and did not purchase it, or it was not purchased for your use only, then you suck.

Publisher © Chelle Bliss December 26, 2025
Edited by Lisa A. Hollett
Proofread by Read By Rose & Shelley Charlton
Cover Design © Chelle Bliss
Cover Photo © Wander Aguiar

MEN OF INKED SINNERS SERIES

Book 1 - Crave

Book 2 - Want

Book 3 - Need

Book 4 - Wish

Book 5 - Desire

… and more to come

To learn more please visit

menofinked.com/sinners

The Men of Inked Sinners series is also available in
discreet paperback & hardcover editions

PROLOGUE
ZOEY

WHOEVER SAYS childbirth is beautiful is wrong.

I begged my sister to let me be in the delivery room with her. She even made me get on my knees before she finally caved and said yes.

I thought it was going to be magical, something like I've seen in the movies. But nope. Not even a little bit—unless the movie is a gruesome horror film.

"Ma, maybe we should stand over there." I point to the chairs near the top of the bed, instead of the end where we're standing.

I've seen my sister's body before, but never, and I mean never, have I seen every single inch of her girl parts on full freaking display. And the number of people coming in and out of her room while she's wide open is shocking and horrifying.

"No, honey. I want to watch my first grandbaby be born," Mom says, gripping my hand tighter to keep me from moving. "This is so beautiful."

"Delusional," I mutter under my breath.

"Zoey," Mom chastises me, sounding exactly like she did when I was a little kid mouthing off. "What's not beautiful about this?"

Well, for starters, her hairy bush. At least that's how I want to answer, but I'm not dumb enough to speak those words aloud. My mom is sweet, but I think that would've earned me a smack to the back of the head. So instead, I say, "Are you serious? Maybe you need glasses."

I'm pushing it now. I know I am, but I can't help myself. I'm acting like a child, but this is traumatizing on so many levels.

But this has made me realize I am never having a baby.

CHAPTER 1
ZOEY

"WHAT'S HE LOOK LIKE?" Lulu says, trying to push me out of the way.

"Why does it matter?" I ask with my back plastered to the door to block her path to the peephole.

"Hot neighbors can be fun, and Lord knows, you need a little of that in your life."

"I'm not sleeping with my new neighbor."

She straightens, finally stopping her lackluster attempt at pushing me aside. "I know. You're not sleeping with anyone. Your vagina is out of business. Store closed. No new customers. Pretty soon, I'm going to put you in a nunnery."

"Is nunnery even a word?" I ask, raising an eyebrow.

My sister is dramatic. She always has been, and I don't think she'll ever change. We balance each other out, though, because I'm the least dramatic person in a very dramatic and over-the-top family.

"I'm going to start calling you Sister Zoey."

I roll my eyes. "I remember plenty of times when you took breaks, and after…" I almost say his name, but it dies on my lips as my body shakes as if the memory of that night is bubbling to the surface.

"Not all men are shit, Zo. Not all men are like him."

I know she's right. Looking at the men in my own family tells me there are good apples out there in the world. But I'm the problem. My ability to pick ones who aren't total jerks is off. I feel like even if they wore a shirt that had *Loser* printed on it, I'd still go straight for them because I'm a glutton for punishment.

That's why it's better if I steer clear. I've been successful lately, but I don't know how long my resolve will last.

"I just needed a breather, Lu," I say with an exasperated sigh.

"Well, you've breathed, and now it's time to jump back into the dating pool. Our plan to become single spinsters and die as roommates kind of shit the bed when I met Oliver."

"Just because you found someone doesn't mean I will." I let my shoulders fall forward, allowing myself to relax a little, even though this conversation always makes me tense.

My sister, being the jerk she is, uses that moment to hip check me, causing my body to jolt to the right. She squeals like she just won the lottery and doesn't hesitate to press her eye to the peephole.

"Didn't Grandpa ever tell you not to do that?"

"Do what?" she asks, her palms plastered to the

wood as she tries to line up her eye with the small opening.

"Use peepholes. They're dangerous."

"Grandpa is a little extreme. Oh, wait." She gasps. "I see him." She presses her face closer, as if somehow that's going to give her a better view, even though I know it doesn't because I've tried. "Oh my God, he's so, so…"

"I know. I know," I mumble.

I nearly swallowed my tongue when I first saw him. The man is easily six feet tall, dark hair, muscular—but not a ridiculous amount—and he can wear a pair of blue jeans like they are made just for him. I couldn't make out the finer details because looking through the peep makes everything appear distorted and extra far away.

"Have you seen a woman?" she asks, still gawking at him.

"Yeah. He's taken, Lulu. You can stop dreaming up a ridiculous fairy tale because it's never going to happen."

She pushes off the door with her nose scrunched. "That's a shame. Maybe they won't work out."

I shake my head as I stalk away from her and head toward the kitchen to crack open a new bottle of wine. "I'm not going to hope they break up. I'm not ready for a relationship either, Lu. And there's no way in hell I'd ever date my neighbor. That can only lead to a disaster. I've had enough drama to last me a while."

"Do you think he has a bike? He looks like he does,"

she asks as she grabs an empty wineglass from the kitchen island.

"What does it matter?" I fill her glass first and then my own as she studies my face. "Nothing is going to happen. I'm closed for business, remember? And he has a woman."

"Don't let that shithead chase you away from a chance at happiness. He doesn't get to do that to you. He's done enough damage. Don't give him your entire future too."

"Jesus, Lu. I haven't even had a sip of wine yet, and you're getting way too heavy, way too fast."

As I lift the glass to my lips, my sister staring me down, she says, "Oliver has a friend—"

"No," I say before she can finish the statement. "Absolutely not."

Lulu grunts her frustration.

I glare at her over the rim of my wine. "Did you like it when Mom tried to set you up with men?"

"No," she snaps.

"Then why are you doing it to me now?"

She plops onto a stool like I've stuck a pin in her and caused her to deflate. "I want to see you happy."

"I am happy. I have the bar, I have my own apartment, I have an adorable niece, and a nosy sister. What else could a girl want?"

"A really big dick," she says simply.

I can't help but burst into a fit of laughter.

Lulu said those words with the straightest face and like it is the most obvious thing in the world. She isn't entirely wrong. I've also had some big ones, but they were attached to idiots who had no idea what to do with them. Shame, really.

But my laughter immediately dies when there's a knock on my front door.

Lulu and I stare at each other with wide eyes.

"Did you invite someone over?" I whisper.

"No. You?" she whispers back.

I shake my head as my eyes move to the door.

"Maybe it's him," she says, waggling her eyebrows.

I wave her off, not wanting to hear anything else about the sexy man who's going to be my neighbor for the foreseeable future.

"I'll get it," she says, hopping off her stool like her ass is on fire and moving toward the door before I can round the island.

"Lulu," I warn, using the best impersonation I can muster of our mother's voice. "Don't."

She yanks open the door, and it's like my feet become glued to the hardwood floors.

There he is.

The new neighbor, oozing sexual appeal. His blue eyes don't land on my sister, but find me across the loft, and I instantly feel the heat of his gaze.

I nearly swallow my tongue as I soak in his rugged handsomeness, something most of the guys in our neighborhood are missing.

There are three types of guys in our area—the stuffy businessmen who wear nothing but designer suits and way too much cologne, the frumpy dudes who don't care about style and look like they haven't washed their hair since the last full moon, or the people who ask for change every time I leave the building.

He's wearing a formfitting black T-shirt that hugs every dip and swell of his muscles, a pair of dark blue jeans that are snug, no doubt making his ass cheeks look like they're ready for a pair of teeth to sink into them, and the outfit is rounded out by a pair of black boots with the laces barely tied.

"Hey," my sister says, peering up at him.

Lulu isn't short for a woman, but this man makes her look small. And not just short, but like she should shop in the petites section of our favorite department store.

He lifts a hand to the back of his neck, giving us a view of the tattoos that curl all the way around his arms. "Sorry to bother you…"

"No bother," Lulu says, glancing over her shoulder at me. "Right, Zoey?"

I blink a few times, snapping out of my lusty haze. "Right," I mutter, barely able to force the word out of my suddenly dry throat.

His fingers curl around the back of his neck and knead, causing all the muscles in that arm to ripple and flex.

My mind is instantly flooded with made-up images of him fully nude and those arms wrapped around my middle or my thighs as he holds…

"I'm moving in next door," he says, not realizing we've been watching him and already know.

"Welcome to the building," Lulu says.

"Thanks." He smiles, and my entire insides melt, because damn it, why is he so pretty?

"My sister lives here. Just her. Not me. Not a husband. Only Zoey."

I grind my teeth as his eyes snap up to me and flash with something I'm not sure I can pinpoint.

What in the hell is my sister doing? He's probably married, and the last thing I need is a flirty neighbor who's also a cheater.

"I'm Hunter," he says to me, not her.

Of course he is. He doesn't look like a Charles, Phillip, or William. Naturally, he has a cool name. No man as ruggedly beautiful as he is could have a basic one. It's like his future was predestined at birth, and his parents knew to name him something fitting for the badass handsomeness that would grace him for years.

"Me likey," Lulu mumbles, but Hunter doesn't seem to hear her.

"A jar fell off my counter and spilled, but I can't locate my vacuum or broom among all the boxes. Do you happen to have either one I can borrow for a few minutes?"

"Sure," I say as I find my footing and push myself away from the island to grab what he needs.

"We have book club every month if your wife is looking to make new friends in the building," Zoey tells Hunter.

I nearly trip over my own feet because I know what she's doing, and there's no doubt in my mind that he knows too. Then there's the simple fact that we do *not* have a book club meeting every single month. Hell, we never have one.

"No wife," he answers.

"Do you want to come to book club?" she asks without skipping a beat.

"Lulu, leave the man alone," I tell her as I grab my cordless vacuum from the charger. "He's busy."

"Book club sounds fun. Once I'm moved in, I may be interested," he says as I hold out the vacuum to him. "Depends on what you like to read."

I could kill my sister. I haven't read a book in the last few months, and I know it's been well over a year for her. We also don't enjoy the same reads. She's more of a thriller and mystery girl, while I inhale all things fantasy and romance.

"We can talk about it another time," I tell him as I offer him the vacuum.

He reaches out to take the vacuum, and his fingers graze my own, electricity instantly zapping through me. Damn. I need to get a grip. A simple touch shouldn't have my entire body coming alive, but my self-imposed hiatus from men isn't doing me any favors right now.

I can't seem to uncurl my fingers from the handle as I stand there, staring at him like I'm in a trance.

His blue eyes bore into me, and it dawns on me that he's not moving either. It's like we're both stuck in this moment, staring at each other like the secrets of the universe are inside the other's eyes.

"Is it hot in here?" Lulu says.

I blink, breaking the weird connection. "Sorry," I

whisper and clear my throat as I pull my hand away, giving him the vacuum.

"Thanks for this. I owe you," he says.

My gaze roams around his face, soaking in every detail. I memorize the stubble high on his cheeks, which meets the dark beard that frames his face perfectly, making those blue eyes stand out more than if he were clean-shaven. His lips are full—the hair neatly trimmed around them as if he's waiting to be kissed.

"It's not a problem," I say and shake my head, and the movement isn't a response to his statement but a silent chastisement of myself for fantasizing about this man in front of him.

"Hunter!" a woman yells from the hallway.

Lulu raises an eyebrow. "Girlfriend?"

"Sister," he replies with a smirk.

"Nice," Lulu whispers.

"I gotta run. We'll talk soon," he says to me, and I nearly melt into a puddle of goo on my wood floor.

When he turns around, my vacuum in his hand, my gaze drops to his ass, and I immediately go weak in the knees. I know plenty of men who are ass guys, but I think it's rare for women to fixate on that part of a man. However, it's the number one thing that makes my heart go pitter-patter. I hate the saggy-jean trend that has gone on for far too long. I want to know what they're hiding in their denim, and this man has everything on full display.

Lulu sticks her head out into the hallway, waving at someone. "Hi," she says.

I groan and nearly crumple to the floor in embarrassment. "Lulu, close the door," I tell her and scrub my hands down my face. "How embarrassing."

She closes the door and gives me a hopeful smile. "That went better than I could've imagined. The man is smitten."

"He's not smitten, weirdo."

"He's into more than just your vacuum. He wants you to—"

I hold up my hand and stop her dead in her tracks. "Don't say it."

"Who was that, Hunter?" his sister asks him, not realizing the doors are thick, but they suck at dampening any sound from the hallway.

"My hottie neighbor's sister," he replies, and my heart beats in double time.

"A hottie next door, eh?" the woman says. "I love that for you."

But before we can hear his answer, there's a click, and all sound from the hallway ends.

"That blush on your face has me thinking I should put your reservation at the nunnery on hold."

I clear my throat as I head back to the kitchen and my glass of wine that I need now more than ever. "It's not happening, Lulu. Stop thinking whatever it is you're thinking."

"I think you're going to get laid soon."

I roll my eyes as I lift the wineglass to my lips. "Nope. You're wrong."

"I've never been so right."

I don't want to tell her that a big part of me hopes she is.

CHAPTER 2
HUNTER

"ARE you going to be okay here?" Lizzy asks as she wipes her forehead with the back of her hand.

"Liz, come on. It's me. Why wouldn't I be?"

She eyes me as she purses her lips. "You've never lived in a big city like this, and you've moved away from everyone and everything you know."

"And you think, what? I'm going to get mugged or crash out every day and become depressed?"

She shakes her head as she grabs a box from the top of the stack at her side and sets it on a lower stack for better access. "No."

"I'm more worried about you on a daily basis than you need to be about me in the *big* city." I use air quotes when I say big.

My sister is always worried about me, about herself, about life, about everything. She's a worrier. I don't know how she even functions with the amount of stress she puts on herself.

She jams a knife into the taped seam and tears

through the box like she's gutting a fish. I don't know if it's impressive or scary with how flawlessly and effortlessly she does it too. "It's just a big move, and it's not like you picked this city yourself. You didn't have a choice."

"Exactly. There was no other choice than to move here. I plan to make the best of it too."

"I know she's going through a lot, but she's a jerk for moving away from you in the first place."

Lizzy still can't bring herself to say her name. She never liked Natalie, especially how things ended with us. The final nail in the coffin was when Nat announced she was moving out of state and taking our daughter with her.

I wasn't happy about it, but I wasn't going to get into an extended court battle that would cause more harm to our daughter than the trauma she'd already been put through with our divorce.

I made the choice to go wherever she did to be close to my little girl. I'd move heaven and earth for her, and that includes moving to Chicago to make sure I am in her life and won't miss a thing.

"What's done is done," I tell her.

My sister shakes her head. "You're too nice sometimes, Hunt."

"All that matters is Amira, Liz. If she's happy, I'm happy. She deserves two parents who aren't at each other's throats all the time. Natalie may be the one going through treatments, but Amira is living through the stress and uncertainty right along with her. I want to do whatever I can to make her life even the slightest bit easier."

I'd already planned to move here in the spring, but when Natalie called and told me she'd been diagnosed with leukemia and was starting treatment immediately, I sped everything up and made the move in two weeks. She needs my help, and Amira needs me around because life is going to change dramatically for her too.

"You're a good man and a good dad."

"That may be the nicest thing you've ever said to me, Lizzy."

She waves her hand at me. "Why are you standing around? Move some boxes. I can't stay longer than this weekend. And I don't know where all these things came from, but you have a lot of everything."

I move quickly, grabbing a box and tearing into it. "I don't have that much stuff."

She grunts. "All of these boxes would say otherwise."

We work in relative silence besides streaming my sister's new favorite songs. It's not my type of music, but I can appreciate it for what it is…noise.

After twenty minutes of not talking, she finally breaks the seal again. "So, the neighbor…"

"Not happening."

A smile spreads slowly across her face. "I don't believe you, and you deserve some fun."

"I'm not here for fun."

"Maybe you can be friends."

I pin her with a stare. "How many female friends do I have?"

"None because you sleep with them all, but I think it's possible—if you can keep it in your pants for any period of time. You could use a friend around here. Someone to look out for you when I'm not around."

"And the neighbor is a good idea because…?"

"Because, what's the term you used?" Lizzy taps her lips like she's trying to remember, but my sister forgets nothing. "The hottie next door."

And she is that. The woman is an absolute stunner. But sleeping with her would be a huge mistake. If we didn't end well, which likely we wouldn't, I couldn't just up and move. And the last thing I want is to share a wall with my ex.

"I can appreciate her beauty without wanting to date her."

Lizzy raises an eyebrow, knowing me better than anyone else in the world. "You haven't been on a date since her."

I somehow stop myself from rolling my eyes. "Natalie."

"Yeah, her. She was the last."

I can't argue with her. She's right. I thought Nat would be my forever, and when she told me she wanted a divorce because she fell in love with someone else, I was beyond devastated. But looking back on things now, all the signs that she'd started having an affair were there, but I was too in love with my wife to believe she had eyes for anyone else but me.

It didn't help that I had just lost my parents in a tragic car accident, a drunk driver crossing over the center line and killing them on impact. I was so mired in my grief that I had ignored her needs, and she found someone who met them for her.

It's water under the bridge now. Years have passed and, looking back on things, it was for the best.

I hated that Amira was stuck in the middle and was the only true casualty of our relationship falling apart. But I did my best to mitigate the damage by being as present as I could be without living in the same house.

"I'm not ready to get serious with anyone."

Lizzy pulls down all the coffee cups I had organized, not liking how I put them into the cabinet. "Top down, Hunt, or else you'll get dirt and debris in them."

"What dirt?" I ask her, confused.

She ignores my question as she places the coffee mugs back inside upside down. "It's been three years. I think it's time."

"Well, as long as you think it's time," I tease.

She throws a dish towel across the island, smacking me in the chest. "You deserve to be happy."

"And when are you going to get serious with someone?" I ask, giving her the same energy in return.

"I'm too young to get tied down."

"You're thirty-two."

"And you're thirty-five, and we're both single. When you get serious about a relationship, I will too."

"Hello. I've been married before. I have a kid, remember? You're behind."

"We're both starting fresh. You're not ahead in anything."

Our parents' deaths took the wind out of both of our sails. It's hard enough to grieve one person, let alone two. And with my marriage falling apart, I wasn't in the mood to even think about getting involved with someone else. I didn't have the mental or emotional capacity for anything besides Amira and survival. My sister was the same. It's like our lives stopped when theirs did.

"And you're in a new city. It's a completely fresh beginning. Take advantage of that."

"Why don't you move here?"

Her nose wrinkles. "I don't think I'm a big-city girl."

"I think once you see the Magnificent Mile, you'll change your mind."

The one thing I know my sister loves more than being a serial dater is shopping. She has no idea what Chicago has to offer, but I've done enough research about my new home that I know Lizzy will visit often, if not for me, then to shop.

"I'll visit a lot. I need to see my little niece as much as I possibly can."

"She's going to need you," I tell her, not trying to make her feel guilty, but stating a fact.

Amira will need as many people around her who love her as she can possibly get. Nat's parents aren't in her life because they aren't good people. With our parents gone and her parents estranged, Lizzy and I are the only other family she has besides Nat and her current husband.

"I promise I'll be around. It's only a six-hour drive. I can come every weekend."

"Let's not get extreme," I tease her.

"You're a jerk."

"I know, but you love me."

"I do," she says and sighs.

"I'm going to work on your bathroom."

"You sure about that?"

"It's the cleanest it'll ever be," she explains.

Growing up, we shared a bathroom, and we both barely escaped with our lives. My sister is a clean freak and a germaphobe. I'm not either, and that caused more than a few fights when we were kids.

"I'm going to unpack my bedding," I tell her.

"What about the stuff for the guest bedroom?"

"It's in a box on the bed."

"I'll do that after the bathroom. Don't touch it."

"Wasn't planning on it," I reply.

Lizzy wants her bed made a certain way, and no matter how hard I've tried to replicate it over the years, I never get it right. How many ways are there to make a bed correctly? According to my sister, there's only one way, and it's not how I do it.

By the time the sun sets, we have almost all the boxes unpacked, and I am fairly settled into my new place.

"When do you start work?" Lizzy asks, clutching a glass of wine to her chest as she stares out over the twinkling lights of the city.

"Tomorrow night."

"They're lucky to have you. You're very talented."

"But you won't let me do a piece on you."

She looks over at me and smiles. "I've been thinking about that lately."

"What?"

"I think I want something to memorialize Mom and Dad. Not as big or as intricate as what you have, but something delicate and meaningful."

"I can work on some designs."

"Yeah. Maybe." She sniffles, and I know the pain of losing them is as fresh and biting to her as it still is to me.

They say time heals all wounds and that, in time, the sorrow of loss fades, but it's bullshit. You just get used to the pain. It becomes your new normal.

"Give me a bit, and we will work on it until it's perfect."

"If I am ever going to put something on my skin, it should be for them."

I chuckle a little, trying to lighten the mood. "You know Mom hated tattoos, Lizzy. It's not the way she'd want you to memorialize her."

"She had one on her ass. Did you know that?" she asks, like we're talking about the weather and not a revelation about my own mother.

My gaze snaps to hers. "What?"

Lizzy laughs softly. "She told me about it once. It was a small heart just above her ass."

"Mom had a tramp stamp?" I'm flabbergasted. Never in a million years would I have thought my mom had something like that.

"Dad liked the look of it."

I blanch a little, hating to think about them sexually even if they're no longer breathing.

"She said it made him happy. She lost a bet with one

of her girlfriends and had to get one because of it, and that's what she chose."

"How come I never saw it?" I ask in disbelief. If I didn't know my sister better, I'd say she was totally pulling my chain.

"I never saw it either. It was right above her crack."

I bristle just thinking about my mom's butt crack. "You're lying."

"I'm not. She said it was just an outline of a heart and it was below the line of her swimsuit and pants, so only Dad got to see it."

I didn't think there was anything new to discover about my parents, but obviously, I was wrong.

"What else do I not know about?"

Lizzy shrugs. "I thought you knew about the tattoo."

"No. Why would she tell me?"

"Since it's your profession, I thought maybe she'd share."

"Why did she tell you?"

"She used it as a reason to tell me never to get one. She said it's forever and not to make dumb bets like she did because they could follow you for your entire life."

I guess you never really know a person, especially your parents. Sometimes it's easy to forget they're more than a mom or a dad. They had an entire life before you took your first breath. They were once young and dumb, making crazy decisions because they were living life for the first time, just like you did.

"Did Dad have a mysterious tattoo too?" I ask her,

figuring my sister somehow has way more dirt on our parents than I ever did.

"No, but he had a piercing."

I stagger back and clutch my chest. "What?"

"Just like you," she says, her eyes dipping downward.

"You're shitting me."

She giggles before she takes a sip of her wine, leaving me to have a mild panic attack.

"Please tell me you're lying."

"I am," she says around the rim. "Can you imagine if he did?"

I wince, unable to even think about it. "No."

"You're a much hipper dad," Lizzy says.

"Hipper?"

She shrugs. "You're covered in tattoos and have more piercings than I do."

"It's not hard to beat having only your ears pierced."

"You have more metal in your body than someone who's had a hip replacement."

"You're ridiculous."

"Where's the lie? Maybe you can share your love of metal with that hottie neighbor."

I shake my head. "I can't risk it."

"Pity," she whispers and moves her gaze back to the nighttime skyline.

It is a pity because the woman next door is exactly my type. But I don't want to mess up my fresh start before I even get settled.

"I need more wine. Want a refill?" she asks.

I know I'll regret it tomorrow, but I say, "Yeah. Sure. What'll it hurt?"

But I know I'll wake up with a headache that will follow me throughout the entire day.

"Good, because you know I don't like to drink alone. Want to watch a movie?"

"Which one?"

"*Goonies*."

"I'm in," I tell her, because watching entertaining and equally bad movies from the eighties is our thing.

"I'll get the wine while you make the popcorn," she tells me as she stalks toward my kitchen.

"Somehow I got the shit end of that stick."

"You make it better," she says. She has always used that as an excuse not to be the one staring at the microwave to make sure it doesn't burn.

I rest my ass against the counter as I press start on the microwave. I love this loft, which is something I could've never found in our small hometown. There's something about this place, this city, that already feels like home.

CHAPTER 3
ZOEY

"CAN'T you buy a fake tree like everyone else in this world?" my cousin Mason huffs out as he fights to get the most beautiful evergreen I've ever seen into the elevator.

"But it wouldn't have the smell," I tell him.

Lulu chuckles. "You can stick one of those car air fresheners on the trunk, and voilà, the smell and the look without all the hassle."

I glare at my sister, both of us ignoring Mason as he continues to struggle because the damn thing is so big. "It wouldn't be the same, Lu."

She picks at her nail, chipping the black polish off her thumb. "Close enough, though."

"Fake pine doesn't smell like real pine," I argue with her.

"Little help over here," Mason begs between grunts.

"I got you," a man says before the tree lifts and is easily maneuvered into the small space.

My gaze moves toward the voice, finding my handsome new neighbor. Lulu's eyes must find him at the exact same moment because her bony elbow jams into my side.

"Hey," he says to me with the hint of a smile.

"Hey," I say back.

"All settled in?" Lulu asks him.

"Pretty much."

"Nice," she says. "New to Chicago?"

I glance down, knowing she's fishing for information when I haven't even bothered to put a lure on the hook.

"Yeah. It's going to take me a while to figure things out."

"Zoey can help. She's lived here her entire life."

I don't use my elbow like my sister. I jab her hand with my nail. Quick and sharp. She's a nosy little jerk.

His eyes move to me. "Your entire life?"

"Yeah," I reply.

"We all have. Our family has lived in this area for generations," Lulu adds, because obviously, my answer didn't go into enough detail for her.

I can't imagine living anywhere else, especially not moving to another big city. It would take me a decade to learn where all the best restaurants are, and I don't have the patience for that. "If you have any questions, I'm right next door."

My statement earns me an approving smirk from Lulu, but luckily, this time, she doesn't add anything more to my sentence.

"That's good to know. Hey," he says as the elevator

dings as it passes between floors, "did you get your vacuum back? I left it by your door."

"I did. Thanks."

Mason hisses. "Risky just leaving things outside. Someone could've swiped it."

"Who's going to take it? Old Ms. Carver in 12S? She can barely see or walk," I ask him, shaking my head. "Don't listen to him. The building is safe."

"I'm Mason," my cousin says. "I'm the favorite cousin."

"Completely our favorite," Lulu says, sucking up because Mason loves it. "And sometimes our muscle."

"Always your muscle," Mason says as he holds out his hand to my neighbor.

"Hunter," the handsome man says, shaking my cousin's hand. "You want help getting this out of here?"

"Aw," Lulu says in a teasing tone, "they're making friends."

"Shut it," Mason says to her before he responds to Hunter. "That would be great."

"We're decorating it tonight if you'd like to join us for a few drinks and maybe some laughs too," Lulu adds.

I glare at my sister as the doors to the elevator open on our floor. I can't believe she just invited him over. They're not helping me decorate. They never do. Lulu's too much of a perfectionist, and Mason has other plans —he always does.

"What are you doing?" I mouth at her with my eyes narrowed.

She waves me off. "We're starting around seven."

Hunter hoists the bottom of the tree trunk off the floor. "I can't tonight. I have to work, but thanks for the invite."

"Pity," she whispers as she follows the guys off the elevator, and I'm left there gaping at her audacity.

It shouldn't shock me, though. She's always been more outgoing than me, but she's never tried this hard to find me a man or push one on me.

"Another time, maybe," Hunter says, barely out of breath as he helps to carry the ungodly large tree I picked out.

"Next year, you're getting a smaller tree," Mason says as he stalks down the hallway behind Hunter, with Lulu hot on his heels.

"The space is too big for something smaller," she tells him. "We tried it once, and it looked ridiculous."

"Who cares? No one sees it," he grumbles.

"I do, and I love having a Christmas tree. If I could keep it up all year, I would," I say, reaching into my pocket to get my keys.

"You could, though. Some people decorate it for every season," Lulu tells me. "But you'd need a fake tree."

"I like the sound of that," Mason says.

Hunter peers over his shoulder at me, and I nearly trip over my feet again. Damn it. Why is he so handsome? It's annoying. And if he's anything like Mason, he knows he is too.

I squeeze around Lulu, Hunter, Mason, and the tree to unlock the door. "You can go once we get inside. I already have the stand set up, but we can get it from here," I say.

"Sweet," Mason says behind me.

There's a thwack followed by, "Not you, dumbass," from Lulu.

"I'll help get it upright before I go," Hunter says as I open the door and step aside, giving them as much room as possible to get the branches through my narrow doorframe without damaging anything.

Lulu's at my side as Mason and Hunter wrangle the tree, getting it into the stand much easier than Lulu and I have been able to in the past.

"He's perfect for you," she whispers.

"Why? Because he's cute and his ass looks good in jeans?"

"I mean, there's nothing wrong with those two things. They're bonus points, for sure."

"That doesn't mean he'd make great boyfriend material," I argue.

"It's a starting point."

"Your bar is far too low," I tell her.

"You need to have a bar, a jumping-off point, or you're going to be alone forever."

"I'm okay with that."

Her shoulders instantly sag forward. "I don't want you to be alone forever. I want our kids to be around the same age, and I've already had one. You're falling too far behind."

"Do you talk to Mason like this?"

Lulu rolls her eyes. "No."

"How's this?" Mason asks, standing near the tree, giving it a look like he grew the damn thing himself.

"It's perfect," I tell him and step away from my sister and her guilt trip. "Thank you both so much for doing this for me."

"Did I even have a choice?" Mason asks.

"A you're welcome isn't too hard," Lulu says to him.

"Thanks," I say to Hunter and ignore Mason, feeling the awkwardness of the energy between us but knowing we have an audience.

"Anytime. I'm right next door if you need anything else," Hunter says to me.

It seems like he wants to say more, but he doesn't. He moves toward the door, and I follow him, feeling my sister's and cousin's eyes on my back.

"Thanks again," I say as he reaches for the doorknob.

"Sure," he says and smiles at me.

My insides liquefy immediately. It's been a long time since a man and a simple smile have had that effect on me. I lift my hand and wave, momentarily dumbstruck and terrified at the same time.

Once the door clicks closed and I turn back around to face my cousin and sister, they're staring at me with eyebrows raised.

"Him?" Mason asks.

"Him," Lulu answers. "He's perfect."

"Perfect?" Mason winces. "Hardly."

"Look at how pink her cheeks are. She's smitten."

"He looks like an angry lumberjack," Mason says.

"Exactly," Lulu replies.

I clear my throat, finding my sanity again. "He's my neighbor."

"Easier access," Lulu says to me with a smirk.

"I slept with my neighbor once. Worst mistake of my life." Mason shakes his head before scrubbing his hand back and forth through his hair. "Don't do it. Learn from me."

I love my cousin, but there are no life lessons he can teach me. The man fumbles through everything and usually lets the wrong part of his body make his decisions.

"I don't plan on doing it," I tell him. "I'm not interested in dating anyone right now."

"Who said anything about dating?" he asks.

Lulu grabs her phone out of her jacket pocket and stares at the screen. "I have to run. Oliver sent a SOS. Harlow blew out her diaper again. That girl is literally full of shit."

Mason grimaces like he's never heard anything so gross in his life. "I never want kids, man."

"It's not so gross when it's your own kid," Lulu tells him.

"I'll never believe that," I say.

Mason chuckles. "She can serve that lie all day, and I'll never believe it either."

Lulu hugs me and then Mason before she pulls on her gloves and heads out the door.

I turn to my cousin, hoping he'll stick around for a bit. "I'll make you dinner if you want to help me decorate."

He stares at me for a minute. I know he'd rather

have his fingernails torn out than decorate a Christmas tree, but I also know he loves to eat and he has an affinity for my cooking.

He draws in a deep breath like he's working through pain along with the answer. "I'll put the topper on."

I stare back at him, knowing I don't want to haul the ladder out to get to the top. His height is useful for that, and in all honesty, he's awful at decorating everything, and that includes the tree.

"You have a deal, but you have to prep the food."

"Do I have to do the dishes?" he asks.

I shake my head. "No."

"You're the best cousin ever."

"Don't let Lulu hear you say that."

He chuckles. "I say the same thing to her."

"We know. Trust me. We know."

He does a good job of making us both feel like we're the most important cousin to him. It's never been a competition, but Mason's male gene needs to make everything a game with a clear winner.

In an hour, we're sitting at my kitchen island with a plate of steak, homemade mashed potatoes, and sauteed zucchini. The tree topper is on and working, and all that's left to do is everything else. I'll be here all night, but it'll be worth it when it's done.

"Dating anyone?" I ask him between bites of steak.

"No. I was digging this one chick, but I found out I was one of many dudes in her arsenal."

"How did that feel?" I ask him, knowing damn well

he's treated women the same way for years and never gave it much thought.

"I hated it. I'm over casual. I want something real and deep."

"Maybe try not to sleep with them right away," I tell him. "Get to know each other first. Build a base on something other than sex."

The man looks pained at my words. "I don't know if I can do that," he admits.

"You can. Maybe if you meet the right one, it'll be easier than you think. Maybe your priorities will shift."

He leans back in the chair and sets his fork down on the side of his plate. "My priorities have already shifted. I didn't need to be abstinent for that to happen."

I jab my fork into a piece of steak and wave it in his direction. "When you stop letting your dick guide you, you'll find what you're looking for."

Mason gazes down at his lap. "He needs to be happy first. If he ain't into her, I'm not into her."

"Most of the time, he's going to guide you the wrong way. You want instant gratification or something lasting?"

"Both is preferable. So, the neighbor?"

"Don't you start too," I tell him, narrowing my eyes. "What does my dad always say? Don't shit where you eat."

"Who's talking about shitting? And that saying is disgusting." He blanches. "It's been a while since you've dated someone. I've noticed, which means it's been too long."

I stare at him. "I'm on a break. I was focusing on

finishing school, and now, with my new job...I don't have a lot of time to devote to someone else."

"Bullshit," he coughs. "I get it, though. Men are trash."

"Not all men," I tell him, but besides the ones in my family, I'm not sure I believe my statement. "But trusting isn't easy for me since..."

"I know, cous," he says with a sad smile. "Someday someone will earn your trust again."

I want to believe him, but I'm not sure about that. It feels like an impossible hurdle that, no matter how many times I try, I'm not sure I'll ever get over again.

CHAPTER 4
HUNTER

THE WIND STINGS my cheeks as I stalk down the street with my hands inside my coat pockets. I've lived my entire life in a cold climate, but nothing could've prepared me for the frigid temperatures of Chicago.

When I open the door and step inside, ready for my first day of work, I've never been more thankful for central heat.

"You're here," my new boss says, rising from the chair behind the reception desk.

"Sorry if I'm late," I tell her as I shiver, throwing off the last bits of chill.

Her eyes move toward the clock on the wall. "You're not." She smiles at me, making me feel like I made the right decision to work here.

I've worked in some shit places over the years, and walking away from my last job wasn't easy. I loved the people I worked with and I had an established client base, but I didn't have a choice because Amira needed me.

"Are you ready for today? You're booked up, but I kept it light, so you only have three customers tonight."

"Great," I say, rubbing my hands together to bring my joints back to life because I'll need them functioning for the next few hours.

"Hunter," Timber says, striding out of the back room. "Good to see you again, man." He holds out his hand to me as he gets closer.

I've known Timber and the owner of the shop for years. We'd talk every time we were at conventions, but never in a million years did I think I'd be working with and for them.

"Lookin' good as always, man." I shake his hand. "Excited to get started."

"That's the attitude I like," Tate, the owner of Inked, says to me.

"Tate's awesome, but you already know that."

Tate stands a little taller, obviously loving the praise. "Don't stop on my account."

Timber shakes his head and laughs. "Just sprinkle a few compliments around her every day, and you'll be good."

"I'm not that easy," she says to him with a pointed stare.

"Sweetheart, you are," Timber says to her with a wink.

"Are you two a…"

Tate waves her hand in the air. "Oh God no. I'm married and not to him."

"Tate's not my type," Timber replies.

"Do you have a type?" she asks him. "Because I think your requirements are breathing and boobs."

Timber shrugs. "Maybe younger me. But older me…"

"Bigger boobs," she says, knocking him with her shoulder.

I can't stop a dumb smile from creeping across my face. I'm glad to know their easy friendship extends outside the conventions where I spent time with them before. I don't want to work in a place where attitudes collide and there is nothing but drama.

"Brains are more important to me now than they were before," Timber says, scratching his cheek through his thick beard.

"He's lying," Tate says to me. "You'll see. Anyway, let me show you your area, and you can get yourself settled. You have about thirty minutes until your first client is here."

"Great," I tell her, shrugging off my coat, starting to overheat from all the layers.

I follow Tate to the back area of the shop, still as brightly lit and beautiful as the front of house. She really did an amazing job making the space comfortable and visually stunning at the same time. It's very different from every single tattoo spot I've worked in previously. Maybe it's because it's a big city and the clientele is expecting an elevated and modern experience.

"Coats and things can go in the back. There's a closet we all share." The heels of her boots that look like they're more for a night out dancing than a snowy winter evening in the city click along the hardwood floor. "Do I need to go over how to keep your area clean and sanitary?"

"No. I'm good there."

"I figured since you've been in the business for so long, you'd know the routine."

I suddenly feel ancient. Tate's younger than me, but she's experienced in the profession and has made a name for her shop outside of her family's reputation. The Gallos are known all over the country for their main shop in Florida. They've been featured in every tattoo magazine, and there isn't a tattoo artist who doesn't know their name.

"Here you go," she says as she stops at the spot where I'll be spending most of my time when I'm at work.

The area is larger than many I've had in the past. Plenty of room to move around while working since some of the angles can become more like acrobatics for me and my clients. The overhead light is a nice soft color and won't leave me with a raging headache at the end of the night.

"I've fully stocked you up, and everything else is as you left it when you stopped in this morning before I came in. You need anything else?"

I shake my head. "No. I don't think so. I think I'm good."

"Hey, Hunter," Melanie, another artist I've met before, says as she strolls to her station with a roll of paper towels in her hand.

I give her a chin lift. "Hey, Melanie."

"Where was I?" Tate asks and pauses for a moment. "Everything else is in the back room, like I showed you when you came to interview and talk to me about a spot. Help yourself to anything in the fridge except what's marked with a name. You eat them at your own peril. After work tonight, we're heading to the place across the street for some pizza and beers. My family owns it. You're more than welcome to join us."

"I may. Is it good pizza?" I ask as I throw my coat over my chair.

"Best in town, but I'm biased."

"Deep dish?" I ask.

She wrinkles her nose. "Uh, no. They don't do deep dish, but it'll be the best pizza you'll ever have in your entire life."

"I'll be the judge of that," I tell her, but I've never had a pizza that has knocked my socks off. They were all just fine and had the same ingredients. Sure, some were better than others, but saying one is the best pizza ever is a lofty compliment to live up to.

"The Gallos know how to cook," Timber says, rubbing his belly in the chair across from my area. "Just don't ask for pineapple on your pizza."

I grimace. "Who in the hell would put pineapple on their pizza?"

Tate touches my shoulder and gives me the biggest smile. "You're going to fit right in," she says before she stalks away and heads back toward the front of the shop.

"I'm glad you gave me a call when you decided to

move here," Timber says as he cleans off the chair for his next customer.

There was no decision. I didn't have a choice of where and when. Natalie made that for me when she moved to Chicago.

"I'm glad you guys had an opening." I drop down into my chair, testing to make sure it'll be comfortable enough and not give me a backache that'll last for days.

"That spot is usually left empty for a guest artist who comes into town, like her family from Florida."

I love that about this place. Not only do I get to work with great people, but I am able to watch masters in the field when they visit. It's a win-win in my book.

The next few hours pass by in a blur. Three tattoos, none of them hard or complex. The tips are larger than I'm used to, but everything about Chicago has been pricier, and people seem to be willing to spend more of their cash, even for a service.

It's nearly midnight by the time we've cleaned the shop, and everyone has their coats on and is ready to sprint across the street before our breath has a chance to form icicles on our beards from our breath.

Although I'd been to the shop a few times before now, I'd never noticed the bar across the street. Sure, I'd zeroed in on the cupcake bakery because I knew Amira would love it, but the bar, I'd totally missed.

I glance up at the sign, *Hook & Hustle*, as we cross through the doorway and enter the bar that's filled with people, which shocks me since it's so late at night. People are eating, drinking, and laughing in almost every seat, and there's a warmth to the bar that no doubt helps make it a favorite of the locals.

I follow Timber, Tate, Melanie, and another artist, Marshall, to an empty booth that's nestled into a corner.

"I'm starving," Melanie says as she pulls off her coat, hanging it on a hook at the end of the booth. "We might need two pizzas."

"Yeah, especially with Hunter in the mix. One isn't going to be enough," Timber adds.

I take off my coat, placing it on top of Melanie's before sliding into the booth next to her. "I only need a slice."

Tate stares at me with wide eyes from across the table. "One is not enough. Not for a Gallo pizza."

"We'll see about that," I tell her.

"We doing a pitcher?" Timber asks.

"To start," Melanie says, rubbing her hands together in a move I know all too well. We're all frozen and will be for the next few months.

"Hey, cousin," Tate says as someone approaches the table.

I lift my head, and my gaze lands on someone I wasn't expecting to see tonight. "Zoey?"

God, she looks good. Her hair's down, the long dark brown strands wavy and flowing over her shoulders. She's wearing a pair of skintight jeans with big chunky winter boots and a sweater with a neck that meets her chin to keep the chill off as much of her skin as possible. She could wear a burlap sack, and she'd still be stunning.

Zoey leans back slightly and stares at me like a deer in headlights. "Hunter?"

"You two know each other?" Tate asks, wiggling two fingers in our direction.

"He's my new neighbor. How do you know him?" Zoey asks her like I'm not here.

"He's my new artist."

Zoey's eyes move to me. "I didn't know you were a tattoo artist."

"Never came up," I reply.

"Wait. You two have had full conversations?" Tate asks, her gaze swinging between the two of us. "He's been in town for like forty-eight hours."

"We've met twice," Zoey tells her. "He needed to borrow something, and he helped Mason carry in my Christmas tree."

I knew from our earlier interaction that Zoey's family was involved. Some people have siblings and relatives they barely talk to, but Mason, Lulu, and Zoey seemed to be as thick as thieves. Kind of how Lizzy and I are and have been since the day she was born. But watching Zoey with Tate, I realized the sharing-is-caring mantra runs further and deeper with the Gallos.

"How cool is this?" Melanie asks. "What a small world."

"It's the Southside, Mel. There aren't that many degrees of separation between people," Timber says to her.

"We live in the big city, Timber. It's not a small town," she tells him.

"We'll talk later," Tate says to Zoey. "We'll take a pitcher and two pizzas with the usual."

"You got it," Zoey says, tucking a lock of hair behind her ear as she sneaks a look at me.

I can't help but turn my head and watch her walk away.

"You like her?" Tate asks, her finger pitched in Zoey's direction.

"I don't really know her."

"She's solid, but my question wasn't *do you know her*. It's *do you like her*?"

"She's easy on the eyes," I say and regret my wording immediately. It's an asshole thing to say.

A sly smile spreads across Tate's face as she slowly leans back until her body is pressed against the booth. "She's single."

"Uh-oh. Tate's playing matchmaker," Melanie teases.

"It's a no," I say quickly, wanting to put an end to the conversation before it even begins.

"Why?" Tate asks, placing her hands on the table, and I suddenly feel like I'm about to be interrogated.

"I don't have time for any complications right now."

"But you're single, right?" Melanie asks. "Zoey's single too. Why do relationships have to be a complication?"

I ignore her as I stare at Tate, wondering what she's going to do because I get the sense that the woman likes to get into everyone's business, especially when it's her own family. "I'm single."

"I saw the way you looked at her," Tate replies. "And the way she looked at you."

"Um, you're thinking something that didn't happen the way you think it did," I lie. I was totally checking Zoey out and wondering if her lips are as soft as they look.

"She's a good girl," Tate adds.

"She seems nice."

"She is. A hard worker too. Most of us didn't want to take over the bar full time when our parents retired, but Mason and Zoey stepped up. They run the joint. Mason uses it like it's his personal dating service, sleeping with way too many customers, but Zoey is very serious about the success of this place."

"That's great," I whisper, and anything else I was going to say dies on the tip of my tongue as Zoey stalks our way with a pitcher of beer in one hand and four glasses curled in the crook of her arm.

"Here you go. I put in the pizzas. It'll take fifteen," Zoey says, and her eyes meet mine as she sets the pitcher down.

I ignore the nagging feeling deep in the pit of my stomach. The one that makes me want to kiss her. To talk to her. To peel back all the layers of Zoey to find out who the woman is underneath. But I have no time for fun. I'm here for Amira, and right now, my needs or wants aren't important.

Lust is just that...lust.

I don't have the time or mental energy to wrap myself up in a woman I barely know. I can't afford to let my focus sway from my daughter to someone else.

There will be a time for me, but for the time being, I'm not the focus, and neither is Zoey, my hottie neighbor.

"You're still having your holiday get-together, right?" Tate asks her cousin.

Zoey nods, pushing up the sleeves of her sweater. "Of course. I always do. You know when it is. I texted everyone."

"Hunter," Tate says, and when I glance her way, she's smiling. "You should come. You can meet some new people. New friends. Hang out with us."

"Maybe. Depends on when it is." Shit. I can't use the excuse that I have to work or that I won't be around. It's too easy for someone to know I'm home since I'm only a wall away. I'd have to creep around my place and be super quiet not to be found out.

"It's next Sunday night," Tate says, clearly already having known it was happening and just finding a way to insert me into Zoey's life against my will. "You free?"

"My sister will be in town," I tell Tate.

"Bring her too," Tate replies without missing a beat.

Fuck. The woman has an answer for everything. "Maybe," I say.

"The more, the merrier," Zoey says before someone yells her name across the bar. "Be back. Yell if you need anything."

Tate and I stare each other down.

When Zoey's halfway across the bar, Timber says, "This is about to get interesting."

[illegible]

CHAPTER 5
ZOEY

TATE'S STANDING at the end of the bar with the empty pitcher, staring at me.

I stalk her way, knowing where this is going to go before she opens her mouth. "Don't say it," I tell her as I grab the pitcher from the bar.

She smirks as her eyes track my moves. "So…Hunter."

The growl that rumbles out of my throat is too low for her to hear over the noise in the bar. "He's my neighbor."

"A very hot neighbor," she adds.

"Obviously," I say as I slide the refilled pitcher back in her direction.

"He's a solid guy."

I glare at her, not wanting to have this conversation with her now or ever.

"I like him for you."

"Well, thank goodness for that. I'm so happy I have the Tate stamp of approval to date a man I never planned on dating and didn't know until a few days ago."

Her face scrunches like she just ate something sour. "You're a brat, Zo."

"I know," I say with a smile.

My entire family is so damn nosy. Sometimes it's funny, but only when it's not directed at me.

"What's up?" Mason says as he slides in next to me, and his gaze moves to Tate and back to me. "This looks tense."

"Hunter," I tell him, tipping my chin in his direction and finding Hunter's eyes on me.

Shit.

Mason's gaze moves to the booth where the Inked crew always sits when they pop in for pizza and beer a few nights a week. "Ah. Nice dude. But why's he sitting at your table, Tate?"

"He works at Inked," Tate tells him.

Mason's head jerks back. "No shit. Small world."

"Small world, indeed," I mutter under my breath.

"I think Zoey should date him," Tate announces like she's somehow in charge of my love life.

"Oh boy." Mason leans back, ready to run because he knows better than to wade into these waters. "I'm out," he says, lifting his hands in mock surrender as he leaves us alone.

"I'm on a break from men."

"Yeah, so was I when I met Wylder," she says. "But be careful, because you could miss something really great that's right in front of you."

"Got it, wise one. Why don't you head back to your people?"

Her nose wrinkles. "You're my people."

"You have thirty minutes to finish before we close," I tell her.

"Fine. We'll talk about him another day."

"No. We won't," I tell her. "You said what you needed to say, and it's over."

She lets out a loud hmpf before she grabs the pitcher and marches back to the table to join her employees.

"Fuck," I mutter, throwing a drying towel over my shoulder to begin cleaning up.

I love my family. I really do, but I could go without them butting into my life for a while. Between my sister and Tate, the pressure is heavy to date someone no one knows. Just because he's new to town and easy to look at, it doesn't make him trustworthy or husband material. They're feral for him for absolutely no reason.

I ignore my cousin's table for the next thirty minutes while Mason and I clean up as the last few customers slowly file out after we cut them off from ordering any more drinks.

Thankfully, the group from Inked left without much fanfare. Tate didn't make a scene, and Hunter gave me a brief and fleeting smile as he exited.

"I think we're good enough until tomorrow. The morning crew can finish," Mason says.

Normally, I'd argue. I don't like to leave anything unfinished, but it was so busy tonight that I am beyond tired. My feet throb with each step, and I can't wait to kick off my shoes and crawl into my bed.

"You take the back, and I'll take the front," I tell him, even though it's been our system for as long as I can remember when we work together. He exits out the back after making sure everything is off and locked, and I do the same with the front entrance.

"Catch ya tomorrow, cousin," Mason tells me.

"Night," I tell him before he disappears into the back, and I glance around the clean dining room before heading toward the door.

I pull on my jacket before I wind my scarf around my neck, preparing myself to be blasted by the winter air. I don't like the heat of summer, but right now, I am over winter, and it has barely even begun.

When I step outside, I look to the right first. Something I always do. I'm aware of my surroundings as much as I possibly can be in the dead of night.

When I turn my head to the left, Hunter is leaning against the building, foot flat on the brick, and staring down at his phone.

"Hey," he says without looking my way as he jams his cell into a pocket.

"What are you doing here?" I ask, locking the door to the bar as my belly does a weird flip.

"Thought I'd wait for you, and we could walk back together."

"You could've been waiting here a long time," I say, pushing on the door handle to make sure the bar is buttoned up tight and trying to control my breathing.

"I took a shot," he says as I finally turn his way. "I'm still unsure of how to get around, and in the dark, it's even harder. Figured since you know the area so well, it was safer to wait for you than to try to traverse the city alone."

I eye him, wondering if he was worried about getting lost or if he had other reasons to wait for me. "It's pretty much a straight shot to our building."

"*Pretty much* doesn't mean it is," he says as we start down the sidewalk, heading toward home.

"You got me there."

"It's safer for both of us this way, though," he adds, which isn't entirely untrue, tucking his hands into his coat pockets.

"So, Inked," I say as I pull on my gloves, wishing I had moved to a warmer climate years ago.

"I've known Tate for years."

"And you came here because of her?"

"No," he says and shivers. "I had to move for personal reasons, and I called her about a job first before I tried other places."

I want to ask about the personal reasons because I'm just as nosy as the rest of my family, but I don't. It's not my place, and if he really wanted to tell me, he wouldn't have given that basic answer.

"Have you been tattooing for long?"

"About fifteen years."

I nearly trip over my own feet but somehow stay upright. "Wow, that's a long time."

He grips my elbow, trying to help steady me.

"Sorry. I'm a little clumsy." I hope he doesn't realize his answer nearly caused me to trip.

"I know I'm old," he says, dropping his hand from my arm as he keeps pace next to me.

"You're not old," I say a little too quickly. "I was just surprised to hear you've been tattooing so long."

"How old were you when I started? Like ten?"

"Maybe." I shrug. "I bet your work is amazing, though," I say, trying to change the subject.

"Do you walk home alone every night?" he asks as we stride down the sidewalk at a fast clip.

"Usually."

"Is that safe?"

"It's only a few blocks, and yeah, it's safe enough. I've never had any issues, and I was raised here, so I know most people. Plus, in the middle of winter, no one is out this late at night unless they have somewhere to be, like at home in the warmth or at work. Safest season there is in the city."

He laughs. "That I believe. Is it always this cold?"

"Usually colder. You'll get used to it," I tell him as he shivers again. "You need a longer coat, and layering is important."

"Why is it so much colder here?"

"Where are you from?" I ask.

"Ohio."

"It's the tall buildings and the lake. It's like a wind tunnel." My point is proven as we make it to the end of a building at a street corner where the wind is whipping so fast, the ends of my scarf become horizontal. "One more block to go," I tell him.

We don't wait for the signal to stalk across the crosswalk, picking up speed the closer we get to our building.

"Thanks," I say as he opens the door for me, and we step into the warmth of our apartment lobby.

Now it's my turn to shiver as the heat washes over me but doesn't chase away the chill that's deep in my bones this time of year.

"Damn. I hate this," he says as we walk toward the elevator.

I haven't stepped inside my apartment yet, but I'm already dreaming of my bed.

"Why did you move to Chicago? If I had a choice, I'd move somewhere warm," I tell him as we step inside the elevator.

"I didn't have a choice, but I've always loved Chicago, so it wasn't a move I dreaded. I just wish I had come in summer."

I stare at him, soaking in his tall frame even though everything is hidden under layers and layers of clothing. I never would've guessed the man is in his mid-thirties. He doesn't look much older than me.

"The summer will be that much sweeter for you. There's nothing better than the city when the sun is shining and the birds are chirping."

"I hope you're right."

I give him a smile before the doors to the elevator slide open on our floor. "I appreciate the company," I tell him as we walk down the hallway, heading to our units.

"It was my pleasure."

"Standing outside in the cold waiting for me wasn't pleasurable," I remind him. "Next time, if there is one, you can just wait inside."

"I'll remember that," he says as I stop in front of my door, and he does too.

My stomach flutters as we stare into each other's eyes. Any other time in my life, I would've asked him inside or at least made a move to kiss him. He's totally my type, but I'm not ready to get into anything, casual or otherwise. Not yet. I'm not sure I ever will be either.

Trust is a hard thing for me now. Mark made it damn near impossible after what he did to me.

"Sleep well," I tell him while I fish out my keys and slide one into the lock as I glance in his direction.

"You too," he says, his eyes roaming my face like he's having the same thoughts I am.

There's a crackle to the air and time seems to slow, but I do everything in my power to ignore the pull the universe seems to have on me toward him.

"Night," I say, rushing into my apartment before I do something foolish that I know I'll regret in the morning.

"Night," he says back to me as I slowly close the door, feeling like I can breathe again once all connection between us is cut off.

"Shit," I whisper to myself, hating that I am at this point in my life.

Why couldn't I meet my hottie neighbor when I was still living my carefree and trusting lifestyle? The universe isn't that kind.

As soon as I toe off my boots and hang up my coat on the hook next to the door, I check my phone. There is only one missed text, and it's from Tate.

Tate: *It's time to come back to the land of the living, and Hunter is the one to do it with.*

CHAPTER 6
HUNTER

"DADDY!" Amira yells out as she runs my way.

I crouch down and open my arms, loving her excitement every time she sees me. I barely make it to her level when she smashes into me, wrapping her body around me like she's afraid I'll disappear. "Hey, baby," I whisper against her hair as I lift her into the air.

Amira's almost too big now to hold like this, but I'll do it as long as I'm physically able to because there's nothing better than the love of my daughter.

My eyes find Natalie, staring at us with an unreadable look on her face. If I didn't know any better, I would think it's sorrow or remorse, but Natalie's never dwelled too much in the past or her feelings—especially when it came to me.

"Hunter," Natalie says with a cold edge to her voice.

"Nat," I reply.

Natalie crosses her arms in front of her chest as one of her shoulders droops. "Can you keep her for the weekend?"

"Of course."

"Mommy doesn't feel good," Amira tells me as she skates her fingertips across my beard.

"I packed her extra clothes," Natalie says to me, ignoring Amira's comment.

There was a time when Natalie was my everything, but now, the only thing tethering us together is Amira. Even though we are no longer in love, I've never wished her ill, and I hate seeing her go through something like this.

"I've got everything else covered," I tell her.

I already stocked my place with all of Amira's favorites. The kid is a bottomless pit when it comes to food, and I do my best to make a few healthy choices while also spoiling the crap out of her.

"Thank you," Natalie says, but somehow the words sound bitter coming out of her mouth.

"Text me and let me know when you want her to come back," I tell Natalie, leaving any distasteful tone out of my voice.

Normally, I'd ask her what the issue is, but I won't do that in front of Amira, and I'm going to give Natalie some grace since she's going through a lot right now. I can't imagine navigating something so serious with an immense amount of uncertainty. I know that she's under a lot of stress right now and that I didn't do anything to cause her to have an attitude.

Natalie reaches down and grabs Amira's bag before she walks the short distance between us. "I will," she says to me before she turns her gaze to our daughter. "Have fun with Daddy, bug."

"I will, Momma. I always do."

Natalie kisses Amira's cheek before stroking her hair a few times. "Be a good girl."

"She's the best," I say to Natalie, earning me a flash of narrowed eyes.

Amira can do no wrong in my eyes, and with the limited amount of time I have her, I'm not about to spend any chunk of it discipling her for stupid shit either.

"Ready to go?" I ask Amira as I set her feet back on the ground.

Amira takes my hand, pulling me away from the front of her house as Natalie stands watch. "Let's do this."

I laugh at her very old-school adult saying. The kid is growing up faster than I want. I know in the blink of an eye she'll be talking about boys and trying to sneak out of the house to hang out with her friends. The very thought makes my stomach twist and my heart ache.

"Aunt Lizzy is on her way here," I tell her as I open the car door for her.

Amira fist-punches the air as she lets out a tiny screech of excitement. "Best weekend ever."

Fifteen minutes later, my car is parked, and we're heading up to my new place. "This is fancy," Amira says, glancing around the parking garage that takes up the entire bottom floor of the building besides the lobby.

"It's really not, baby."

"Do you have a doorman? I've heard some buildings have a doorman."

"Yeah. There's one there."

She peers up at me as she takes my hand. "Can we go see him?"

When I don't immediately say yes, the kid pours it on thick with a pouty face that makes it impossible for me to turn her down. "Only for a minute. We'll grab my mail and then let the man work."

"Perfect," she says, almost skipping with every step.

At this age, the smallest things make her happy, and I do everything in my power to make them happen. She deserves happiness, especially now, with Natalie being sick.

As soon as I pull open the door separating the garage from the lobby, Walter is nearby and hustles our way. "Well, well, well. Who do we have here?" he asks, staring down at Amira.

"Walter, this is my daughter, Amira. She'll be staying with me from time to time and wanted to meet you."

Walter smiles as he fishes something out of his pocket and holds out a sucker to Amira. "This is for you."

Amira glances up at me, and I give her a nod, before she snatches the sucker out of his grasp. "Do you always have suckers?"

If the kid didn't love the idea of a doorman before, she sure as hell does now.

"Always." Walter pats his pocket as he smiles down at my little girl.

"Best place ever," she whispers as she tears the wrapper off the sucker like an animal.

"Thanks, Walter."

"Anytime, Mr. Evans," Walter says with a tip of his head. "Anything else I can do for you?"

"I want pizza for dinner, Daddy," Amira says between licks of her sucker.

"What's the best pizza in the area?" I ask him. "I haven't explored too many places yet."

"Hook & Hustle has the best pizza, hands down."

Of course they do. "I've been."

"And the pizza was great, right?"

"Yes," I reply because I can't lie to the man. And besides the pizza, it had the prettiest woman I've laid eyes on in a very long time.

"Your neighbor owns the place," Walter adds.

Amira gasps. "You know the owner of a pizza place?"

"Kinda, kiddo," I tell her, but I don't get into specifics.

But I already know the night is going to go to shit. The last place I want to take Lizzy is to the Hook & Hustle because once she lays eyes on my hottie neighbor again, she'll be trying to set us up on a date. But maybe since Amira will be with us, Lizzy won't come on quite as strongly with Zoey.

———

I was wrong. Dead wrong.

"Hey, Hunter. It's nice to see you again," Zoey says, her eyes drifting to Lizzy and Amira. I can see the questions swirling behind her eyes.

From the outside, we look like a married couple with our daughter, but the reality couldn't be further from the truth.

"Hey, Zoey." I smile at her, careful not to let my eyes linger on her for too long.

"I'm Lizzy, Hunter's sister," Lizzy says, giving Zoey a giant smile. "I don't think we've had the pleasure of meeting yet."

"Ah. You're the sister. I'm his neighbor. He borrowed the vacuum from me when he was moving in."

My sister's gaze snaps to my face for a moment. "Ah. The hottie next door," she whispers, hopefully too quiet for Zoey to hear.

If Zoey did hear her, she doesn't let on. "And this is…" Her eyes are pinned on Amira.

"My daughter, Amira," I say, waiting to see some sort of reaction out of her. I never said anything about having a daughter or any kids in general. Not because I am embarrassed or trying to hide anything, but we barely know each other and there wasn't a reason to tell her…at least, not yet.

"Well, aren't you cute as a button," Zoey says as Amira glances up at her and smiles.

"You're the hottie neighbor?" Amira asks.

My heart sinks, and I wish I could go boneless, slink underneath the table, haul my ass out of the bar, and never have to face Zoey again.

Zoey chuckles. "Kids, huh? They say the darndest things."

Lizzy covers her mouth, but her eyes are glistening

with tears of laughter and completely at my expense. "They do," Lizzy replies.

"What do you want to drink?" Zoey asks, totally glossing over Amira's statement.

"A pitcher of iced tea would be great if you have it," I tell her, knocking my knee against my sister's underneath the table.

"Tea would be great," Lizzy says after she clears her throat.

"Perfect. I'll give you a minute to look over the menu," Zoey says, giving me one last look-over before she walks away.

"Well, this is kismet, isn't it?" Lizzy says, her eyes pinned on Zoey as she stands behind the bar.

"What's kiss met?" Amira asks Lizzy as she draws in a blank notepad Lizzy brought with us.

Lizzy finally looks down at Amira and smiles. "It's kismet, and it means fate."

"What's fate?" Amira asks in response.

"It means meant to be."

Amira's eyebrows draw together. "Pizza is meant to be?"

"No, darling," Lizzy says with a chuckle. "It's our waitress that's kismet."

"Zoey?" Amira asks, looking where Zoey is filling our pitcher with iced tea. "I'm confused."

"Just draw your picture, sweetheart. Ignore your aunt. She's confused."

Lizzy stares at me across the table with a raised eyebrow. "You knew she'd be here, didn't you?"

"Yes."

"Been here before?"

"Once," I reply honestly.

"By accident?" she asks.

I shake my head. "We all came here after work. The shop is across the street."

"See?" Lizzy says. "What are the chances?"

"Pretty damn high since her cousin owns the tattoo shop."

Lizzy's eyes widen as soon as the words are out of my mouth. "What? Are you serious?"

I nod. "I didn't know it until we came here after work."

"You're not making a good case that this wasn't meant to be," Lizzy replies.

"It's a no, Lizzy. Drop it."

"Amira," Lizzy says, drawing Amira's attention away from her picture of something that resembles a cross between a dog and an elephant.

"Yeah, Auntie?" Amira says sweetly.

"Do you think Daddy should get a girlfriend?"

My eyes narrow at my sister. She's stooping to a new low, asking my kid about my personal life. I'm sure, in Amira's mind, she'd rather have her mom and dad together than for me to find a new girlfriend.

"Who?" Amira asks without hesitation.

"Here's the tea," Zoey says, placing the pitcher on the table in front of us, along with three cups. "Did you decide what you want to eat?"

"We'll take a large pepperoni and a small black olive for the little one. Both well done," Lizzy replies.

"Excellent choices," Zoey says, and her eyes flick to me. "Anything else I can get you?"

"No, Zoey. That's it." I give her a smile, loving the sweet softness on her face. There's a kindness to her I haven't experienced in many people, but I haven't spent enough time with her to know if it's genuine or a mask she wears in front of others.

"Let me know if you need anything," she says before she stalks away, heading back to the busy bar area.

"She likes you," Lizzy says to me before turning her attention back to Amira. "What do you think of her for your daddy?"

"This is ridiculous," I mutter, scrubbing my hand down my face.

"I like her," Amira says. "And she makes pizza."

That's my kid. Always thinking of her stomach. The apple doesn't fall far from the tree.

My sister grabs the pitcher and starts to fill the empty glasses. "Well, it's settled. You have two yes votes for Zoey."

"Um," I mumble as I lean back in the booth. "I'm a no, and my vote is the only one that counts."

"Daddy, it's time for you to find someone. Mommy has Tim, but you have no one," Amira says, sounding more like an old sage than a little girl.

I wrap my arm around her and pull her closer. "I have you, kiddo, and that's all I need."

Amira curls into my side as her arm comes around my middle. "I'm not with you all the time. I like Zoey. She looks like fun."

"Yeah, she does," Lizzy says, waggling her eyebrows at me.

"Enough of that," I tell Lizzy, giving her my best shut-up glare before looking back at my kid. "How's school?"

"Good. I have a boyfriend."

She says those words as I take my first mouthful of iced tea, and I nearly choke to death on the liquid. "What?" I cough out, pounding on my chest to clear my airway.

"What's his name?" Lizzy asks, like this is normal for a kid Amira's age.

"Bryant," Amira says as she draws spots on the animal.

If I wasn't choking before, I surely am now. Bryant is such a basic, stuck-up prick name. There is no way in hell I'd ever let her be with a guy named Bryant when she is old enough to date.

"Is he cute?" Lizzy asks.

"He's okay. He's nice to me."

Well, Bryant at least has that going for him.

"You know if a boy isn't nice to you, that doesn't mean he likes you, right?" Lizzy asks Amira.

"I know. If a boy is mean, then they're a jerk. But that's not Bryant. He gives me a cookie from his lunch every day."

My sister eyes me across the table as I wipe the tears from my eyes. "Calm down. It's an elementary-school crush. It's about cookies at that age."

"It's always about cookies, no matter the age," I tell her with a flat stare.

"So, I have Bryant, and Mom has Tim, and now Daddy needs someone too. What about you, Auntie Lizzy? Do you have someone too?"

"No, baby. Not yet." Lizzy brushes her hand across the back of Amira's head.

"You need a boyfriend," my kid tells her aunt, and for once, I'm in agreement with her. "Everyone needs someone in their life."

"When did you get so smart, baby?" I ask her, hating that she's growing up.

It's an amazing thing to watch, but also heartbreaking at the same time.

When I gaze across the bar, my eye catches on Mason. As soon as he sees me, he strides across the room. "Hey, man. Good to see you again, but without a tree this time."

I hold out my hand to shake his. "You too. This is my sister, Lizzy."

When I turn my gaze toward my sister, she's staring at him with a look I'm not sure I've ever seen on her face before.

"Hey, Lizzy," Mason says with a smile on his face.

"Hi," Lizzy barely squeaks out.

"I'm Amira. His daughter," Amira says, pitching her thumb at me.

"Nice to meet you, kid," Mason says, giving my kid a wink. "I've got to run. We're slammed. Hopefully I'll see you again soon. Nice to meet you, Amira and Lizzy."

As soon as Mason is a few feet away, Lizzy finally sucks in a breath. "Who is that man?"

"Zoey's cousin," I tell her.

"He's the most beautiful thing I've ever seen."

"Ooh," Amira teases. "Auntie Lizzy has a crush."

Lizzy's back straightens. "I do not. I can appreciate beauty."

"Uh-huh. I saw the way you looked at him," Amira adds.

The problem is, I did too, and it is the same way I look at Zoey. And that means nothing but trouble for the both of us.

CHAPTER 7
ZOEY

TATE: *Did you ask him out yet?*

I stare down at my phone, wondering if my cousin has ESP or a webcam inside the bar. I glance up, watching Hunter, Lizzy, and his little girl.

It hadn't even crossed my mind that he could be a dad. I don't know why it seemed so farfetched, and my jaw nearly hit the floor when he introduced her. A man in his mid-thirties is bound to have one or two little ones running around. Heck, many women my age do too, but I often forget just how old I am at times.

Me: No. I don't want to date.

I sigh, setting my phone down next to me as I refill a beer for a regular.

"You're looking extra pretty tonight, Zoey," Mr. Walsh, someone I've known since I was knee-high, says as I set the drink down in front of him. "Have a special guy yet?"

"No, Mr. Walsh. I'm enjoying the single life."

"Attagirl," he says, giving me a smile that makes the lines near his eyes deepen. "Men are nothing but trouble."

"Your lips to God's ears," I whisper to myself before I notice another text from my nosy cousin.

Tate: Okay. So, just sex. Do it.

I'm surprised her message isn't in the family group chat, using the power of numbers to gang up on me. Peer pressure in my family is a real thing, and it is often used and successful.

Me: He's a dad.

I don't know what fatherhood has to do with anything, but I am running out of excuses that satisfy anyone.

Tate: It means he knows what he's doing.

I groan as soon as I read her words.

Me: I don't know him.

Tate: I have for years. Solid dude. Good dad. Talented artist. I wouldn't push you toward him if he were a shithead.

That is true. My cousin knows what happened to me. If she had any doubts about Hunter, she wouldn't tell me to date him either.

Me: I'm not ready.

Tate: Who is? I wasn't when I met Wylder. The man was like a bulldozer to my cold, dead heart.

"Zoey," another regular calls out, lifting his hand in the air to further get my attention.

"What's up, Chuck?" I ask as soon as I'm close enough for him to hear me easily over the noise of the crowd.

"Dirty martini with extra olives." Chuck smiles, showing off his missing tooth.

And I don't know why, but the blank space always puts a grin on my face. Chuck's an ex-pro hockey player. Someone my Uncle Vinnie knows from years back since they were both former professional athletes with deep roots in the area and well-known to every Chicago sports fan.

"You got it," I tell him before I walk away, sneaking a peek at my phone before I make his drink.

Me: I don't think he likes me.

Tate: Don't be ridiculous. What's not to like?

"He keeps looking at you," Mason says as he comes to stand beside me with a handful of dirty glasses.

"Who?" I ask, not bothering to look at my cousin, keeping my attention on the task at hand.

"Hunter," he says plainly as he places the empty glasses in the sink between us.

My heart beats a little faster in my chest. Too fast, really. I shouldn't care. It doesn't matter if he is looking at me or not. We aren't a thing, and I don't see a path for us in the future either.

"And?" I ask, my voice dripping with annoyance.

Mason hip checks me, nearly causing me to spill the vodka. "He likes you, and somehow I'm okay with that."

I drop the little spear with three olives into the drink before I turn my full attention toward my cousin. "Does it matter if you're okay with it?"

"I'm your cousin."

"Uh, yeah, cousin. Not my father," I remind him. "I don't need your approval."

He lifts his hands as he jerks his head back. "Touchy, touchy. What's your problem?"

"Everyone's in my business."

"Welcome to my world, Zo. You two have been bossing me around my entire life. But I'm not telling you what to do, just stating a fact. The man likes you."

"And you're okay with that because…?"

"He seems like a nice guy." My cousin's gaze swings toward the table across the bar where the three of them are sitting. "Look at them. They genuinely like each other, and based on how his kid is interacting with him, he's not an asshole. You need someone who's a nice guy."

Nice guys have never been my thing. That's how I got myself in this pickle to begin with. The bigger the asshole, the more I liked them. Enter Mark, a guy I had a fling with until he violated my trust in a way no man ever should.

"I'll mark you down for a yes, then, to go along with Tate."

"Tate?" he asks, raising an eyebrow. "How does she factor into this?"

"Remember, your sister is his boss," I tell him before marching away with Chuck's drink. "Sorry for the delay."

"No worries," Chuck says, lifting the drink as soon as I set it down. "Mason hassling you?"

Part of me wants to say yes, but I know Chuck

would give him shit all night, and Mason doesn't really deserve that. "No, he's just being Mason. Family, am I right?"

Chuck hums his agreement. "Try having five siblings."

"Five?" My body recoils in shock. I can't imagine raising one Chuck, let alone five more. "Your poor mother."

"The woman's going straight to heaven with all of our bullshit she had to put up with when we were little." Chuck laughs and shakes his head. "Hell, we're a lot to handle even today, but somehow, she takes it all in stride. I think we broke her spirit a long time ago."

"No doubt," I tell him. "Holler if you need anything else."

"You got it, kiddo." Chuck smiles again, lifting his glass toward me in thanks before I saunter away and back toward the middle of the bar, where Mason is still standing.

"You want to take them their check?" I ask him as I print out the bill.

"No, that's all you," he says, stalking away.

"Asshole," I mutter and shake my head.

As soon as I head toward their table, my gaze lands on Hunter, and his eyes are pinned on me. I swallow hard, trying not to stumble over my own two feet because there's something about the way he looks at me that's alarming. Not in the murdery kind of way, but in the way that says he'd make my toes curl.

"That pizza was phenomenal, Zoey," Lizzy, his

sister, says before I have a chance to place their bill on the table.

"Thanks. It's not hard to love something covered in cheese," I reply with a smile, sliding the bill into the middle because I'm not sure who's paying.

Hunter snags the slip of paper before his sister has a chance and turns it over, reading the amount.

"Tomorrow, I'd like to get the best Chinese food the city has to offer. Any recommendations?" Lizzy asks. "I tried to do a quick search, but there are so many options."

"If you want the best, you have to go to Chinatown," I tell her as I try to stand still but fail. I can feel Hunter's eyes on me, and it's completely unnerving.

Lizzy gasps. "There's a Chinatown here?"

"Yes, and it's not far from here either," I reply.

"This is amazing," she says, looking to her brother. "Maybe you picked the right city after all."

"The city has a lot to offer," Hunter says.

My gaze dips to him, and my body instantly heats at the way he's looking at me.

I clear my throat as I glance over my shoulder, needing to break eye contact with Hunter. "I gotta get back to work. Mason needs my help," I say as I'm about to run away to the safety behind the bar.

Hunter reaches into his back pocket and fishes out his wallet as his sister continues to talk. "Before you go, do you have a favorite restaurant in Chinatown?"

"The Evergreen," I tell her. "It's at the end of the street and has been my go-to for years."

"Perfect," Lizzy says. "Thanks."

"Do they have fried rice?" Amira asks, looking between Lizzy and me.

"Of course," she tells her as she taps Amira on the nose.

I glance down again because I'm a glutton for punishment, and when Hunter's looking right at me, I can't think, but I nearly run away like an idiot.

CHAPTER 8
HUNTER

MY BACK ACHES from a night of tossing and turning on a mattress I haven't broken in yet. I rub at my side, looking down at Amira as she draws a heart on a piece of paper.

"I'll take out the trash," Lizzy announces as she pulls the bag from the bin.

"What?" I blink a few times and shake my head, swearing I heard her wrong. My sister has never taken out the trash, not even when we were kids. "Why?"

"It needs to be done," she answers plainly, like I've lost my mind for even asking.

"When are we going to eat?" Amira asks, not looking up from her drawing.

"In a bit, baby," I tell her. "We'll head down to Chinatown in a few hours."

"A few hours isn't a bit," she argues, sounding way older than she is.

"We just had lunch," I explain.

"It's three."

I loved the period before now when the kid couldn't read a clock. Time didn't exist to her, and I could pull the wool over her eyes sometimes, but now, she watches and times everything, including eating.

"Be right back," Lizzy says as she slides on a pair of slippers.

When the door clicks and she disappears, I get a niggling feeling that makes all the hairs on the back of my neck stand up.

I stalk toward the door, wondering what my sister is up to because she always has something going on in her brain.

"What are you doing, Daddy?" Amira asks from the kitchen island.

"Nothing," I mutter as I press my ear against the wood.

"Doesn't look like nothing," she replies in her sweet tone, but she's calling me out and I'm not a fan.

I hear a distant knock and then silence for a beat.

"Hey," my sister says. "Sorry to bother you."

"Hi, Lizzy. No bother. Is something wrong?" Zoey asks.

I shake my head at my sister's boldness. It's not surprising. It's how Lizzy's been her entire life. She sticks her nose where it doesn't belong. I used to get mad about it, but I've come to realize her actions come from a good place, even if the execution leaves a lot to be desired.

"Do you hear something out there?" Amira asks as she stops drawing and sits up a little straighter.

"Your aunt is talking to someone."

"Who?"

"Zoey."

"I like her," Amira says as she goes back to her artwork. "She's nice and pretty too."

"Yeah," I mumble. "She is."

"She likes you," she adds, like she's fully grown and knows what she's talking about.

"How can you tell?" I ask.

"We're heading down to Chinatown in a bit, and we were wondering if you'd like to join us. We're not sure where to park or how to get there and figured we'd ask the expert. Plus, it's always good to have friends in a new city, and I thought we could get to know you better," Lizzy says to Zoey.

"Well, um, I…" Zoey stammers.

"It's okay. Maybe another time," Lizzy replies.

"No. Wait. I can go."

My heart flips, and I instantly growl, upset with my body for having a reaction to her response.

"Give me an hour to get ready. I'm a hot mess," Zoey replies.

"Babes," Lizzy says, "if that's your idea of being a hot mess, I can't imagine what you think of me."

"You're stunning," Zoey says.

"Well, so are you. Take as much time as you need. We were going to leave around five so we could walk around for a bit before we have dinner."

"I'll be ready," Zoey says.

"Excellent. See you then," Lizzy says.

I hurry away from the entry before my sister has a

chance to open the front door. I take the seat next to Amira, pretending to study her art masterpiece.

Lizzy strides in with her head held high as she kicks off her shoes. "I ran into the neighbor," she lies.

"Which one?" I ask, playing dumb.

"Zoey." Lizzy toys with the end of her braid, a habit she's always had when she's nervous about something. Good. She should be.

"And?" I ask, waiting to hear more of her nonsense.

Lizzy moves toward the island and leans over, placing her hand in her palm as she stares at Amira's drawing instead of looking me in the eyes. "We were talking about Chinatown, and I invited her along."

"Really? And what did she say?"

"She was excited to be invited."

If I didn't know better, I'd think my sister was telling the truth. All of it rolled off her tongue so easily that I never would've questioned a word.

"Daddy was listening at the door," Amira says, ratting me out.

"Hey," I say, glancing down at my little girl, who's always supposed to have my back but likes to stir the pot a little more than most.

"Asshole," my sister mutters.

I place my hand against my chest and raise my eyebrows. "I'm the asshole?"

Lizzy nods. "Why were you eavesdropping?"

"Why were you sticking your nose where it doesn't belong?" I shoot back. This isn't our finest adult conversation, but no matter how old we are, we're still siblings with all the bullshit that comes along with that relationship.

"I want to get to know her better."

"Lizzy," I warn, but I don't know why I waste the energy. Lizzy's going to do what Lizzy wants to do, and everyone else be damned.

"I want to know about her cousin, okay?" she asks, blinking her eyelashes rapidly like she's somehow innocent.

"That's it?" I ask.

She nods. "Of course. What did you think?"

I stare at her, and she stares back. "I don't trust you."

Her lips crack into a smile. "Smart. Smart."

"You like her cousin?" Amira asks Lizzy.

Lizzy nods. "He's cute."

"Do not mess up the relationship with my neighbor because you have the hots for a man you don't even know."

"I'm not going to mess anything up, big brother. And when are you going to admit that you think Zoey is beautiful?"

"Of course she's beautiful," I scoff. "I'm not blind, Lizzy."

"And you like her too?" Lizzy pushes. A little bit is never enough for her.

"She's my neighbor and my boss's cousin. Let's not forget that fact."

Lizzy crosses her arms as she cocks her head. "And?"

I sigh, scrubbing my hand down my face. Exasperation doesn't even begin to describe how I feel in this moment.

"I like Zoey too, Daddy. I approve," Amira adds.

I forget that she's at the age where she's listening to everything and absorbing it. She's not too little to understand what's going on or to fully comprehend what we're saying.

I peer down at the small human I helped create, wondering where my little girl has gone. "You do?"

"She's nice. What's not to like?" Amira asks.

I shrug. The kid has a point. When you're young, things are really that simple. Adulthood complicates everything, and sometimes it sucks.

"Yeah, Hunter. What's not to like?" Lizzy asks, taunting me.

CHAPTER 9
ZOEY

"WHO WAS THAT?" my sister asks when I pick my phone back up from the counter.

"Lizzy."

"Lizzy?"

"Hunter's sister."

She clicks her tongue and follows it with a few hoots. "And?"

"And what?"

"What did she want?"

"She wants me to go with them to Chinatown for dinner."

"I hope you said yes."

I sigh as I pour myself another cup of coffee, barely awake even though it's the afternoon. "I did."

"Excellent. What are you going to wear?"

"It's not a pageant, Lulu."

"It's a date."

"It's not," I fire back as I lift the coffee mug to my lips. "A date doesn't consist of his child and sister."

"It's the closest thing you've had to a date in a long time. What are you going to wear?" she asks again.

"Jeans and a sweater," I answer, knowing she won't relent unless I give her something.

"The red sweater."

"No."

"Yes. The red sweater."

"The gray one."

"You look too washed out in the gray one."

"I've got to go," I tell her.

"Wear the red one," she says again.

"Byeeee," I call out before I hit the end button, silencing the ridiculous conversation.

I wouldn't admit it to my sister, but I am going to wear the red sweater. I have two hours to make myself presentable. I barely slept last night because I was over-tired, and today, I look more like a zombie than a human being.

Somehow, I am ready by the time there is a knock on the front door. Here goes nothing.

———

"This is Chinatown," I say, turning around to face the three of them.

The look of shock on their faces is immediately evident. Wide eyes. Gaping mouths. Silence. Living here my entire life, I forget not every city has its own China-town. And Chicago's is elite. It isn't half-assed with a few Chinese restaurants. There are more restaurants than you could eat at in a week, along with stores selling all types of goods. The signs are in Chinese. It feels like you are stepping into another world, and I love everything about it.

"Wow," Lizzy says, blinking a few times, like her eyes are betraying her. "This is…"

"Amazing," Hunter whispers as he reaches out, taking Amira's hand.

"They have fried rice," she says with the biggest smile on her face as she glances up at Hunter.

"They do, sweetheart," he tells her.

Lizzy stalks up to me and loops her arm in mine. "Thanks for coming," she says as we start to move again, winding through the people dotting the sidewalk.

"I'm hungry," Amira whines from behind us.

"Let's get the kid fed, and then we can explore," Lizzy says, and I can't disagree with her.

Am I in the mood to eat yet? No. But do I want to make the kid starve because my stomach hasn't caught up with the fact that I am awake and need nourishment? That is an even bigger no.

"Is the restaurant far?" Lizzy asks.

"No. It's at the end of the street," I explain.

"I'm glad my brother has such a sweet neighbor."

I give her a tight smile. She's exactly like Lulu, sticking her nose where it doesn't belong.

"Hunter likes to pretend he wanted to move here, but he really had no choice. Natalie didn't think about anyone except herself when she decided to relocate. She ripped Amira out of the cute little life she had in our small town and plopped her right into the middle of this big city."

"I can't imagine moving as a kid or even as an adult. This has always been my home. It had to be hard on her."

"Kids are resilient. She's done well with the move and seems to love her new school. But I worry about Hunter. It's harder to make friends and connections as an adult. This wasn't a move he made by choice, but out of necessity. He wanted to be by his child."

"I respect that." I motion toward the sign above the door to the Evergreen. "We're here," I announce.

Amira practically bounces as she lets out a little screech. She's a kid after my own heart when it comes to food. I've been a foodie my entire life, and the variety of cuisine, along with the sheer number of restaurants, in Chicago makes it all possible.

The restaurant is busier than I thought it would be at this hour. Half the tables are full, and there's a small crowd waiting to be seated.

"This place smells amazing," Lizzy says as she stands at my side while we wait to talk to the hostess.

"It is. Best in town," I tell her as my stomach grumbles, coming alive once again.

There is a bit of awkward silence as we wait, but as we're walking to the table, Amira announces, "Daddy, I want to sit next to Aunt Lizzy."

"Whatever you want, you get," Lizzy tells her, not letting Hunter answer.

We're brought to a booth, and my belly flips a little

at Hunter's proximity as we slide into our spots across from Lizzy and Amira.

As soon as we take off our coats, I can feel the heat radiating off him. The man is like a furnace, which would be nice to have beside me on a cold winter night.

Don't go there, Zoey.

I clear my throat, trying to pull my thoughts back to the present. Food. Sister. Little kid.

"Is Mommy going to be okay?" Amira asks out of nowhere.

Hunter sets down his menu and looks at his little girl. Lizzy freezes, her eyes wide as they lock on her brother.

"She'll be okay, sweetheart," he tells her with a soft, sweet tone, but his body is as rigid as a bowstring.

"Is she going to die?" she asks, staring down at her fingers as she picks at her nails.

My heart squeezes in my chest, and I realize there's something going on that I'm totally clueless about. Maybe that's why Hunter moved to Chicago. They dropped hints, but I hadn't picked up on it completely until now.

He reaches across the table, placing his hands on top of hers. "She's doing everything in her power to get well again, Amira. The doctors are working as hard as they can to make her better," he replies.

Amira sniffles as she hangs her head. "She's so sick, Daddy. Almost every day, she's too tired to do anything, and she barely eats."

My eyes begin to water. Kids see everything,

whether people think they do or not. They hear it all too. No matter how hard we try to hide things to spare them the misery, they know.

"That's from the medicine. Her body's using all her energy to make her better," he explains.

"Miranda's mom died," Amira says.

"Who's Miranda?" Lizzy asks, wrapping an arm around Amira's shoulders.

"A girl in my class," she tells her aunt as she leans against her, needing the physical comfort.

"Sometimes things happen, sweetheart," Hunter says after pausing for a moment.

I wouldn't even know where to start with this conversation. How you can be honest with a child and not scare the living daylights out of them is beyond me or my maturity level.

My thoughts slip to my uncle Angelo, along with Tate and Brax. They were so young when they lost their mother to cancer. I don't know how he dealt with everything. Maybe Hunter could talk to Angelo since my uncle walked the same path decades ago.

I don't know why I do it, but I slide my hand over to Hunter's, hidden away under the table, and squeeze.

He immediately squeezes back, almost deflating, like my mere touch helped release some of the pent-up tension inside him.

A woman walks up to the table, interrupting the difficult conversation and asks to take our order. But for some reason, I don't pull my hand back immediately.

If I'm honest, holding his hand feels natural, and I

also don't want to be rude. I need to pull it back without it being impolite or noticeable to the two people across the table from us.

"Veggie fried rice," Amira says first, not giving anyone else a chance to order. She's adorable and reminds me so much of myself when I was little. The smile on her face is nice to see after such a heavy conversation.

"I'll take the same," I tell the waitress. The last thing I need tonight is to be weighed down by a lot of food.

Hunter and Lizzy order next, and I can feel the tension return as soon as the waitress walks away. We're all waiting for Amira to ask more questions about her mother's illness, but to our surprise, she doesn't.

"You know who likes fried rice?" Amira asks, glancing up from the drawing she's working on.

"Who?" Hunter asks her.

"Bryant," Amira answers.

"Fuck my life," Hunter whispers.

I glance at him and find a pained look on his face. "Who's Bryant?" I ask him.

"My boyfriend," Amira replies in a sugary-sweet tone, not realizing how much that answer bothers her father.

Ah. First crushes. I remember mine from elementary school. Anthony Garabaldi. It lasted a week, and we never even had a chance to hold hands. He dumped me because Sara Wexler shared a brownie with him. It didn't take much back then for love to bloom. Just a little dessert.

And thank goodness first crushes don't turn into

long-term relationships, because I've run into Anthony over the years, and I dodged a huge bullet.

"He shares his cookies with her," Lizzy explains.

"That's sweet of him," I say, giving Amira a smile when she glances up at me again. "Boys don't usually like to share their sweets."

"Not you too," Hunter says, shaking his head.

"Hey, you guys are usually the ones taking the cookies and not the ones to share them. So, maybe Bryant is one of the good ones," Lizzy replies.

"I have to agree with your sister," I tell him, holding in a giggle because this entire conversation is upsetting to him, which is understandable.

I remember how upset my dad was about every single boy I liked when I was a kid. The man was always in a panic, but between Lulu and me, we wore him down over the years.

Hunter rolls his eyes and lets out a grunt. "You two have a very low bar."

"What does a bar have to do with it?" Amira asks her father.

"It's hard to explain," he tells her.

"It means it doesn't take much to make us happy," Lizzy says, answering the question easily, unlike Hunter.

"Cookies make me happy," Amira replies.

"You're just like your daddy," Lizzy says as she leans over and places a kiss on top of Amira's head.

I give Hunter's hand another squeeze and release my grip, sliding my hand over to my side of the booth while Amira and Lizzy are focused on each other.

Hunter turns his head, staring at me for a beat, and from the look on his face, I'd say he didn't want me to do that.

And the problem is, I didn't like letting go of him either.

CHAPTER 10
HUNTER

"I HEARD YOU WENT TO CHINATOWN," Tate says as I sit at my station, prepping for my first client of the day.

"News travels fast," I say, not surprised by that in the slightest. "It was a nice time."

Tate slides across the area on a wheely chair she grabbed from someone else's station. "Did you ask her out yet?"

"No."

Her eyes narrow on me, and she gets in my personal space and drops her voice. "Why not?"

I huff out a sigh as I tear off a sheet of paper towel. "We barely know each other."

"But I know you and I know her, and it's perfect. I don't usually stick my nose in where it doesn't belong, but—"

Timber lets out a loud laugh, causing Tate to turn and glare at him. "I'm not sure you've ever said something so funny and unbelievably false before, Tate. You *always* stick your nose where it doesn't belong. That's why we love you so much."

"It's the Italian in me," she says.

"It's the Gallo in you," Timber replies. "They're all nosy as hell. You'll see. I've never met a family so in each other's business. And they're the absolute worst at keeping secrets too."

Tate glares at him. "I think it's how all families are. We're not abnormal."

"I don't tell my family shit. We all have our secrets, and we know better than to let one slip. Sure, my family can't keep a secret as a collective, but we all have our own individual secrets and know better. You guys…" Timber shakes his head. "You share everything, and I mean *everything*. Word to the wise, Hunter, if you're gonna date the cousin, Tate will know everything too."

"Are you bitching about my family? You seem to love them when you're scarfing down their meatballs and pasta," Tate says to him.

"Best meatballs ever, and I do love them, but I don't know if I could deal with everyone knowing my business all the time. My family is as tight-lipped as they come."

"I'm sad for you," she says to him. "If you can't share the deepest, darkest parts of yourself with the people who are supposed to love you the most, who can you share them with?"

"I keep all the deep, dark shit to myself," he tells her. "The way it was meant to be."

Tate just shakes her head. "Ignore him. Anyway, what's taking you so long?"

"I'm not in the right headspace, Tate," I tell her, finding the entire conversation weird because she's now my boss. When we were only friends, this would've been an easier conversation, but now, my employment hinges on too much.

Tate leans back in the chair, crossing her arms in front of her chest, and studies me. "Zoey isn't Natalie. And all that shit went down in a bad way. It wasn't your fault, and you deserve to find someone who's going to love you in the good and the bad. I mean, those are the vows we take, yeah?"

Sometimes I forget how long I've known Tate and that she knows a lot more about my life than anyone else does. Maybe I felt there was a safety in telling her things when we'd only see each other at tattoo conventions. There was a level of anonymity in the distance of our friendship back then that isn't there now.

"Yeah. Some of us believe them, and some of us don't," I reply, grinding my teeth as I tear off a few more sheets, making a pile.

"Zoey wants someone who believes in those words too. I'm not going to get too into your business…"

"Too late," Timber mutters, but he scurries away in a hurry when Tate throws a wicked glare at him from across the room.

"But when I see two people I care about and know are perfect for each other, I can't help but say something. And I promise, if shit goes bad, it won't have any bearing on your job here at Inked Southside."

Famous last words. I've heard that shit before from friends who have set me up with people they knew, and as soon as it ended, I never heard from the *friend* again. Even if it wasn't my fault when things fell apart after a few dates. Shit always gets too complicated, and lines blur until there's nothing left.

"I'll think about it," I tell her, hoping it'll be enough for her to drop the subject, even for a short time.

The smile on her face is instantaneous. "Good. That makes me happy."

"If you're happy, I'm happy," I reply.

"What do you have to lose, Hunter?" Tate says as she uses her feet to propel herself and the chair back to its original location. "She might be your perfect match."

I continue prepping, milling over everything Tate said. Could Zoey be a great match for me? Absolutely. Am I ready for that level of commitment? Part of me wants to say yes, but I made a promise to myself that I'd put Amira first, at least for a little while longer.

I need to give my daughter my full attention, pushing aside everything I may need for now. When things settle down and Natalie finishes treatment, I'll think about opening my heart again and dipping my toe back in the dating pool.

"What are you doing for dinner tonight?" Tate asks as she walks by, carrying a box of new T-shirts she ordered for the front of the shop.

"I was going to grab a sandwich from down the street."

"You can come with me. My family does a small dinner every Monday at the bar."

"Can I come?" Timber asks.

"No." Her answer is immediate. She doesn't even look at him when she says the word.

"Jerk," Timber mumbles. "A meatball, at least?"

"I'll bring you two," she replies as she drops the box onto a waiting room chair. "Happy?"

"Very," he tells her.

"I don't know," I say to her.

"Everyone here has been there. I'm not asking you to do something they haven't done themselves. I promise to behave. We won't even talk to Zoey."

I eye her, and although she looks sincere, I doubt she'll keep that promise. "Fine. I'll drop in for some food."

"Good. You should have enough time between your second and third client. They're small designs to start, but your third will take you the rest of your night."

"Great," I mumble. If I didn't have a backache already, my night would end with one.

Melanie pops her head around the corner from the stock room. "I want a slice of lasagna."

Tate groans. "Fine. I'll bring a box of food back with me. There are always leftovers."

"Maybe Betty will box them up for you," Timber says, rubbing his hands together like he's already dreaming of sinking his teeth into the meatballs he keeps going on about.

The front door opens, and an older gentleman walks in, looking like he's lost. "I have an appointment," he says, smoothing back his hair that has been blown around by the wind.

"What's your name?" Tate asks as she walks around the reception desk to peek at the schedule.

"Luke."

"Ah, Luke. Yes, you're with Hunter today. He's one of our best," she says, giving me what seems like high praise, but little does Luke know, she says that about all of us.

I stand up, walk toward the front of the shop, and hold out a hand to Luke. "I'm Hunter."

"Luke," he replies, taking my hand in his, but his gaze is moving everywhere and nowhere at the same time. "Sorry, I'm a bit nervous." He pulls his hand back, wiping it on his shirt. "I've never done this before."

"Don't worry. We'll go slow," I tell him.

Over the years, I've had more first-timers than I can count. Most of them come back for another tattoo after they realize it isn't as scary as they thought or the pain isn't as bad as they believed.

But Luke is a bit surprising. He isn't like my usual newbies. He's older, probably around sixty. Way older than most of the people who walk in here without any other ink.

I motion toward a waiting room chair. "Do you know what you'd like to get?"

"Something simple," he replies as he slides into the seat next to where I planted my ass. "I'd like a rose, all black ink, along with a name."

"What name?" I ask, wondering if I should give him my speech about adding names to your skin and the curse it usually puts on the future of the relationship.

I wish someone would've given me that talk before

my dumb ass put Natalie's name on my forearm, which has now been covered up as if it was never there.

"Grace," he whispers. "She is my wife. Was." He glances at his lap, his lips curving downward like his eyes. "She passed last year, and I want to pay tribute to her."

"I'm sorry for your loss," I say, my heart aching for this man I don't even know.

"She was the love of my life. I was a lucky man to find someone to love me the way she did, and I'd like to pay tribute to her in some small way. I want to carry a reminder of her on me forever, so when my cold, lifeless body is in the ground, she'll always be with me."

"I can do that for you. Why don't you come back to my station, and we'll pick out a rose design you'd like, unless you have something already in mind."

"I don't have one in particular," he says as he pushes himself up from the chair.

"We'll find you something," I promise him as I stand too, motioning for him to follow me to my area.

It takes a bit longer than I anticipated for Luke to select the right rose. He's picky, but I wouldn't expect anything less for a tribute tattoo to the woman you love and lost.

"What's this going to feel like?" he asks as I'm about to draw the first line.

"Some people say a bee sting, but I don't know. To me, it's more of a light and pinpointed burning. It's not unbearable. You'll be okay, and if you need a break, just let me know."

"My wife passed of cancer. The pain she went

through was more than I ever thought a person could take. I think I'll be fine, Hunter. It can't be any worse than the agony I felt when she died."

I know the grief I went through when my parents died. It's the only thing I can compare to what he must've gone through. I know it's not the same, but the hurt and heartbreak were so deep, I sometimes felt like I couldn't escape it, no matter how hard I tried.

Luke only winces through the first few lines, and I give him time to adjust to the feeling of the needle going into his flesh. He sits in relative silence through the rest, shedding a few tears along the way and apologizing every time he wipes them away.

"You married?" he asks near the end.

"I was, but we've been divorced for a few years."

"Girlfriend?"

"Not yet."

"Don't wait too long to find the right person. Life passes in the blink of an eye, and there's no greater joy than the love of a good woman. I may be filled with utter sadness right now, but I wouldn't give up all the years of happiness we had together to avoid this feeling. Don't waste your present on the past, Hunter. Life's too short."

"Noted, Luke."

"I like you, Luke," Tate says, obviously eavesdropping on the conversation. "I'm trying to get him to ask my cousin out."

Luke glances from her to me. "She hard to look at?"

"No, she's beautiful," I reply.

"Is she mean?"

I shake my head.

"You're wasting time," he says.

"Boss's cousin. It's an issue," I tell him.

"So not an issue," Tate butts in again.

"I agree with her. One date never hurt anyone," Luke adds.

I growl, hating that they're ganging up on me, and it isn't even a scheme they came up with beforehand. "I'll think about it."

"Smart man," Luke says as he gazes down at the fresh ink on his skin.

"You've made your boss very happy," Tate adds, rubbing her hands together. "Now, we need to make a plan. I'll talk to Lulu."

"No," I snap, not wanting anyone else planning out my dating life. "Let me handle it."

Tate lifts her hands and smirks. "I'll keep my nose out of everything," she lies.

I already know she's going to be deep in my business, no matter what she says or how much I beg her not to be.

"This is so exciting," Tate says, almost squealing with delight.

I hope for her sake, and mine, that whatever happens doesn't make my world implode any more than it already has.

Am I upset about being strong-armed into asking Zoey out? Not really. I like her. The moment I laid eyes on her, I wanted her. I'm not an idiot or blind, but am I in the headspace to be a good boyfriend and a good father? I don't know, but I guess we are going to find out.

"Let's just hope she says yes," Timber adds, lobbing that little nugget of anxiety into the mix.

"She will," Tate answers with so much certainty in her voice that, if I didn't know better, I wouldn't question a single word coming out of her mouth.

Luke gives me a small pep talk one more time before he wishes me well, promising to check back with me soon for a full report.

I've never had so many people involved in my dating life—or lack thereof. This will either be the most amazing thing ever or the biggest failure of my life, which is saying something after going through a divorce.

———

Two hours later, I'm sitting at the bar, surrounded by a majority of people I've never met and the biggest plate of food I've ever seen in my entire life.

I'm a big dude, but there's no way I can finish everything they made me take. Even after I stopped filling my plate, their grandmother added more. The woman wouldn't take no for an answer, just like all the women in their family, from what I can tell.

"My dad was a single father when he met my mom," Tate says. "Well, Tilly is actually my stepmother. They met after my mom died from cancer when I was little. And then there's Wylder. He was a single dad too.

Just because you have kids doesn't mean you need to stop living."

"I'm sorry," I tell her, swinging my gaze from the plate to her. "That had to be hard on you as a little kid."

"I was so young that it seems like a dream now, but it makes me understand a little bit about being a single parent and taking the leap to get into something more. My dad was all alone, though, and didn't have an ex-wife to share custody, but that didn't make it any easier."

"I can't imagine," I whisper, and I can't put myself in her father's shoes.

"What are we talking about?" Mason, Zoey's cousin, asks as he sits down with a plate as full as mine.

"Hunter is trying to figure out how he's going to eat all his food," Tate replies.

"You won't. I never do, but that doesn't mean I can say no to my grandmother."

"Everything she made looks so good," I tell them.

Mason chuckles. "Gram didn't make all this. She's not a great cook. She has a few dishes she can do well, but other than that, everyone else did the cooking."

I stare at him, blinking. "But I thought…"

"You thought wrong. The sausage and the eggplant are hers."

The door to the bar opens, and the two girls I know are Tate's stepkids come barreling our way with their father, Wylder, right behind them, another little girl in his arms. Tate slides her chair back, leaping to her feet right in time to open her arms and capture the girls before they knock her right over.

"My girls," Tate says, kissing each one of them on the cheeks. "How was school today?"

I remember when I was able to ask Amira that question in person every day. I miss those times, and I took every single one of them for granted.

"Boring, as usual," the oldest says. "I'm ready for it to be over."

"Just a few more months," Tate tells her, fingering the braid that is slung over the girl's shoulder.

"And then another year," the girl replies.

"It flies by, baby. Don't worry," Tate says and turns her attention to the smaller one bouncing up and down on her tiptoes. "And you, sweetheart?"

"We dissected a frog today," the small girl says with the biggest smile.

Tate's face matches mine as she grimaces. "That's gross."

"I know," the girl says, peering up at her dad. "Dad pretended to throw up when I told him."

Tate chuckles as she leans across the girls to touch her husband's face. "Hey, handsome."

"Hey, doll," he says to her before giving her a kiss on the lips. "Not the thing you want to hear about as you're eating."

"And this one," Tate says, reaching for the little girl in his arms. The tiny thing doesn't waste a moment and almost leaps into her mother's arms.

"She's good. Just woke up from a nap," Wylder tells her, shucking off his coat. "I'm starving. Come on. Let's get you two food, and we can sit down with Mom."

I watch in fascination at how easy it is for Tate with the girls. Or at least, it appears to be.

"So, what's new?" Mason asks me as Tate sits down with Willow in her lap.

"Not a damn thing. You?"

"Nada. How's your sister?" he asks.

I peer over at Mason. "She's good. Back home in Ohio."

"I'm sure her husband is happy she's back," he says as he stabs his fork into a piece of sausage.

"She's not married," I tell him, knowing exactly what he wants to hear.

"Really? She's too pretty to be single," Mason says.

"Oh boy," Tate whispers. "This is going to get interesting."

"When's she coming back?" Mason asks like he didn't hear his cousin's response.

"A few weeks."

"Tell her to come in and say hello."

"I will," I lie with a slight nod.

"He's lying," Tate says without looking in my direction. "No sane man would give that message to their sister."

Mason touches his chest with his free hand, his eyebrows drawn together. "What? I'm a good guy."

He looks truly offended. I have no doubt that he's a good person, but he also looks like so many guys I know who don't make the best partners. While I wouldn't mind him dating one of my friends, dating my sister is a different story.

"You are, Mason. You're one of the best people I

know," she says. "You're my brother and I love you, but..."

"Then what's with the crack about a sane person not letting me date their sister?" he asks her, placing his fork down on his plate.

"Hey," Zoey says, sliding into the seat beside me. "What's going on over here?" When she asks the question, she looks at me like I was the one in the middle of a heated argument.

"Tate doesn't think Hunter would want me to date his sister," Mason says, his voice filled with hurt and a heavy dose of anger.

"Uh-oh," Zoey says, placing her hand on my arm like it is the most natural thing in the world. "I stepped into it, didn't I?"

And by the look on Tate's face, she clocked Zoey's hand immediately.

Shit.

CHAPTER 11
ZOEY

THERE ARE VERY few reasons Mason ever stops eating. Either his plate is empty, or he's upset about something. And by the way he's staring at Tate, it's the second reason, and Hunter's caught in the middle.

"And how many guys, even some of your friends, who wanted you to give me their number… Did you pass along the digits to me?" Tate asks.

"Hell no," Mason snaps.

"Exactly," Tate says, rolling her eyes at her brother.

Mason groans, running his hands down the front of his face before he meets her eyes again. "But that's because they're my friends, and that's a no-go for me."

Tate drums her fingernails on the table as she stares at Mason. "Okay. Let's say it was some random man, would you have done it then?" she asks again.

"No."

Tate lifts her hand, waving it around. "Ding-ding-ding. There you go, genius," Tate taunts him.

"What's going on over here?" Dad asks, coming up

behind me, placing his hand on my shoulder. "You guys are louder than usual."

"Hey, Dad," I say to him, tipping my head upward to look at him. "Mason and Tate are discussing something stupid. Have you met Hunter yet? He's my new neighbor and Tate's newest artist. He's new to the city."

Dad's eyebrows rise. "Wow, really? That's weird."

I don't know why, but the smattering of gray that streaks above my father's ear always makes me frown. When I think about him, the mental image I have always had is of him from when I was a little girl. But every time I see him, I am reminded that time moves forward, and we are all getting older.

"It was meant to be, Uncle. Who knew it was such a small world," Tate says.

"What brought you to town, Hunter?" Dad asks him.

"My ex moved here with my daughter, and I didn't want to live far away," Hunter replies honestly.

"I respect that," Dad says, giving Hunter an honest smile.

From what I've been told, Dad was a player back in the day. I imagine he was a lot like Mason, working behind the same bar, just as cute, all the female patrons trying to leave their number or looking to hook up in the bathroom.

Mom loves to tell the story about the day they met. She says he saved her, and from that day forward, they have always been together. She says she fell madly in love with him. Love at first sight. But I think she embellishes a lot of it because Dad's account of that day isn't all sunshine and roses.

"I'm Lucio," Dad says, holding out his hand to Hunter.

Hunter moves his arm, and I suddenly remember I'm still touching him and pull my hand back.

"Hunter, sir."

My eyes slide to Tate, and she's smiling at me like she caught me doing something I didn't want anyone to see. And she isn't entirely wrong either. Every time I'm near Hunter lately, I touch him without even realizing what I'm doing and let it go on for far too long.

"We're not that formal, Hunter. Lucio is fine. No sir, please."

"Of course," Hunter replies. "Sorry about that."

"Uncle, if I were your buddy, would you have given my number to your sister?"

I blanch at the thought. He's talking about his aunt, even if it is hypothetical.

"You're shitting me with this, right?" Dad asks Mason, staring at him like he's grown three heads.

"I'm not. Would you?"

Dad chuckles and shakes his head before stalking off, giving an answer without really giving an answer.

"Fuck," Mason hisses, picking up his fork again. "I'm a good guy. I want to find a good girl and settle down. I want the marriage and the kids, but everyone treats me like I'm a gigolo or something."

"Did you just use the word gigolo?" I ask, snickering.

"Zip it, Zoey," Mason snaps, stabbing the sausage on his plate like it's the one who hurt his feelings and not everybody else around him.

"Uncle Mason. I want to sit by you," Hazel says as she climbs up into the chair with a juice box in one hand and a cookie in the other.

"At least there's one girl in this family who likes me," Mason grumbles.

"We all like you, you big dope. We love you."

"You're the bestest," Hazel adds, helping to melt any heat Mason is still feeling.

"No, kiddo. You're the best," he says, taking a cookie off his plate and sliding it onto hers.

"I think we missed something," Wylder says, his eyes moving from Tate to Mason. "Do I want to know?"

"No," Tate says, dropping the topic.

"I'm sorry," I say to Hunter, hating that my family sometimes goes a little off-book.

"Don't be. It's just Lizzy and me. Dinners are quiet and boring. This is great. Even better than great."

"That's sad," I say to him, wanting to reach out my hand and touch him again, but knowing we have an audience, and I don't want him to get the wrong idea.

"It is, but even when my parents were alive, it was only us. I never had a big family like this. You've really got something special here."

I glance around, looking at my family. "I really do," I whisper.

"Are you going to be late tonight?" Wylder asks Tate.

"No. I have one more client, and then I'll be home. Probably by nine."

"Will you tuck me in tonight?" Maddox asks Tate.

"Of course, darling," Tate replies.

My chest warms watching them all together. My cousin was so lucky to find a wonderful husband and stellar kids. The girls adore Tate, and she does them, too.

If I am completely honest with myself, I want that too. I just need to find someone I can trust with my heart, along with my body.

Hunter glances at his watch as he takes another forkful of food. "I hate to do this, but I gotta get back to the shop. I have a client coming in a few, and I need to prep."

"I understand," I tell him, but I don't want him to go. It has been nice having him here, even if he isn't here for me alone. "Do you want me to bring some leftovers home for you?"

He stares at me.

I stare at him.

Shit.

Those words came out sounding different than I wanted. My cheeks heat, and I glance down, unable to keep my eyes glued to his. "I mean I can keep them in my fridge until you get home tonight, or you can grab them tomorrow."

"That would be great," he says. "Thanks."

"You're welcome," I mumble, wishing I could crawl under the table and hide.

Hunter says his goodbyes, running out of the bar like his ass is on fire.

"Nice," Tate says as soon as he's out of ear range.

"What?" I ask, pretending to be clueless.

"You two need to go on a date," she says as she holds Willow on her lap, bouncing her.

"That's a no," I say quickly.

Tate stares at me, making me squirm a little in my chair.

"I'm with Tate," Mason says between bites. "He seems like a good guy, and you've had some real shitheads."

"You just want to get closer to Lizzy," I tell him, knowing his game. I've been a witness to it my entire life, and Mason always has an angle that benefits him.

"She lives in another state," he replies.

"My ability to trust anyone outside of this family is almost nonexistent after what happened with Mark."

My cousin gasps and drops his fork onto his plate. "You said his name," he says, his voice growly. "You never say his name."

"I'm trying to grow."

"You're healing," Tate says. "And maybe Hunter has helped in some way. Maybe he's restoring your faith in the opposite sex."

"I don't know," I mutter.

"I've known Hunter for a long time, Zoey, and he's one of the good ones. He's not a cheater. He's not a liar. He's a girl dad who moved to a new state to be closer to his daughter. If you're not going to take a chance on a guy like that, you may as well give up on a happily ever after for the rest of your life."

I sit with her words for a few seconds, wondering if she's right. How many years am I going to let Mark steal from me? He's already done enough damage, and am I willing to give him my entire future too?

"One date. What'll it hurt?" she asks.

"I agree with her," Lulu says, appearing out of nowhere. "I've been trying to make this happen since he moved in, but she's been stubborn."

"*She's* right here," I say, crossing my arms over my chest as I stare at Lulu. "And you're just as stubborn as me. I don't know a single person in this family who isn't stubborn."

"Me," Mason says, waving his fork around. "I'm easy breezy."

Lulu and I snort out laughs.

"Easy might be right, but you're not breezy," I tell Mason.

"What's it mean to be breezy?" Hazel asks, looking at Mason with confusion written all over her face.

"I'm like the wind, doll. I go with the flow," he answers her, wiggling his fingers like he's floating.

"Dad's not breezy," she replies without skipping a single beat.

Lulu covers her mouth with her hand as she snorts again. "Your dad is..." she starts to say, but she's laughing too hard to finish the statement.

"Wylder is like a skyscraper," Tate says, reaching out to touch her husband's hand. "He doesn't move, but the wind goes around him, and I'm good with that."

"I've gotten better," Wylder states. "You can't have three daughters and a wife and not be flexible."

"That's how you got the third kid," Lulu says with a smirk.

"Speaking of flexible, where's your husband?" Wylder asks Lulu.

"He got a call last minute." She sighs and stabs at her pasta like it's offended her in some way. "It's the busy season, and I hate it. I hope he makes it home before midnight tonight."

"Why don't you go with him?" Wylder asks. "You could keep him company in the truck all night."

"Can't do that with the baby. I used to before Harlow was born."

"I can watch her," I say.

All eyes at the table swing to me.

"What? I can watch a baby."

"You never offer to watch her," Lulu says.

"I'm always working at the bar," I tell her, trying to come up with a reason that'll satisfy everyone, even if it's bullshit.

I was starting to get baby fever. But after what I witnessed when Harlow was born, I wanted to bury it as deeply as possible. Especially since I wasn't in a relationship and had no plans on dating anyone in the next decade.

But there is a deep ache that rears its ugly head every time I am around my little niece, and I can't shut up the little voice in my head that says, *You want one of them too.*

"You'd really watch her tonight?" Lulu asks, her eyebrows drawn inward.

I nod. "She can hang with me while I clean up, and then I'll take her home. You can swing by and grab her whenever. I'm up late."

"I've never left her with anyone except Mom and Dad," Lulu says, glancing down at her baby girl. "I don't know."

"It's me, Lulu. I'm not a stranger."

"Do you know how to take care of a baby?" she asks.

I glare at her. "I babysat half of the shits here. I know what to do. She'll still be breathing when you pick her up. You want to spend time with your man or not?"

"Who is this girl before me?" Tate asks from across the table.

I give Tate the middle finger.

"Okay. Just for a few hours," Lulu says, but I know she's nervous. I get it. This is her baby, but she's also my niece. I'd give my life for hers if it ever came down to it.

"I can handle it," I tell her, but I'm not so sure it will go as smoothly as I hope.

Four hours later, we're in my apartment, and the baby is screaming louder than I ever thought her little lungs could.

When the elevator dings, I run to my door, pressing my eye to the peephole.

It's Hunter. My shoulders slump forward in relief as I reach for the door handle, and I run into the hallway with Harlow in my arms.

"Help," I say, bouncing the crying little girl in my arms. "She won't stop, and I don't know what to do."

The alarmed look on Hunter's face softens as he looks down at Harlow. "Gimme," he says, walking toward me with his arms out. "I got you."

And for the first time in a long time, I wonder if he truly does.

CHAPTER 12
HUNTER

ZOEY LOOKS how I felt for the first month of Amira's life. I remember being in a panic over every small cry, wondering what I did wrong. Babies are a guessing game until you figure out how to read their minds or anticipate the problem before it has a chance to rear its ugly head.

I pat her butt, and the diaper is clean. One thing down and a dozen more to go.

"I just changed her." Zoey stares down at Harlow with sorrow in her eyes. "I tried everything. I fed her, changed her, sang to her."

"Can you sing?" I ask, trying to lighten the mood.

Zoey tilts her head and stares at me. "Are you trying to be funny right now? Did I break her?"

"No, babies cry. It happens."

"It happens? Why the hell does it happen?"

I chuckle. Even though it's not funny to her, it's funny to me because I was her years ago. "When all else fails," I say, flipping the baby in my arms so her hands and legs dangle and her belly is flat against my forearm, and I cradle her face in the palm of my hand. Within ten seconds, she quiets.

"What in the sorcery is that?"

"She has a stomachache. Amira used to get them all the time when she was a baby."

"You're a natural," Zoey says, her voice all breathy like she just finished a marathon.

"No, sweetheart. I'm just a dad with experience."

"I don't know why I told Lulu I'd watch Harlow. I don't know what I'm doing."

"Don't be so hard on yourself. Babies aren't easy," I tell her, touching her shoulder. "I was in your shoes once."

She peers up at me with big eyes swimming with unshed tears. "I've never been so frazzled in my entire life."

"Why don't you come in and relax a minute?"

"No. No. I'd better stay at my place in case Lulu shows up without texting first. You want to come over? I have your leftovers and a bottle of wine that's calling our names."

I could say no and go into my empty apartment like an idiot, or I could accept and spend what's left of the night talking to a pretty woman over a few drinks. The extra perk—the baby. I'm a sucker for them, and if things hadn't fallen apart between Natalie and me, I would've wanted more.

"Your place," I tell her, moving to hand her Harlow back.

Zoey holds up a hand, stopping my motion. "No. She's comfortable. Hell, she's almost asleep."

"It's a lot of work, crying that much," I tell her, watching her face light up as she stares at her niece and touches her tiny, pudgy cheeks.

"I hear that," she says, and something pulls at my heart. She strokes the baby's cheek, getting close to her face. "Been there, princess. Tears are exhausting."

And there's something about her tenderness that has my heart beating a little bit faster.

As soon as Zoey turns around to walk back into her apartment, she freezes, and I nearly walk into her back. "What's wrong?"

"Did you send me flowers?" Her voice is so soft, I almost don't make out the last word.

"No, I didn't." I don't bother asking why I would. We barely know each other.

"No one has ever sent me flowers."

"Probably from someone in your family," I tell her, gently bouncing the baby in my arms.

"Maybe my mom," she says before she moves again.

Zoey bends down, grabbing the flowers off the floor with one hand and reaching for the card with the other, and all the color drains from her face as her eyes skim over the words.

CHAPTER 13
ZOEY

"WHAT'S WRONG?" Hunter asks me.

My heart's pounding so fast, I can hear it in my ears. The tiny hairs on the back of my neck and along my arms are standing at attention, wanting to run away as badly as the rest of me does.

Breathe, Zoey.

I glance around, wondering if he's hiding somewhere nearby, watching me.

"Zoey," Hunter says, and his warm hand touches my arm.

I'm not expecting the touch, and I jolt backward.

"Babe, you okay? You look like you saw a ghost."

"Inside," I whisper. "We need to go inside." I say the words, but I don't move. It's like the fear has my feet stuck to the floor and my body on lockdown.

Hunter reaches for the doorknob, opening my apartment door. When I still don't move, he takes the flowers from me and places them back where I found them before he takes the card from my hands and tucks it into his pocket. "Inside," he says, his voice laced with command.

My body drifts through the doorway, through the foyer, and straight to my couch. It's as if I'm on autopilot. Memory overtakes my entire being.

"Sit," Hunter tells me, and I do without a second thought.

Hunter's beside me a moment later, his body turned toward mine, Harlow still over his arm, but I can't bring myself to look at his face. "Who are they from?"

"Mark," I whisper as I twist my fingers together in my lap, trying to calm my mind and give it something else to focus on besides the panic.

Hunter sets his hand on my arm near my wrist, and I don't pull away. There's something about him that makes me feel at peace by his closeness. "Who is Mark?" he asks.

I close my eyes, wishing I could erase that whole part of my life. I was so dumb and careless. I'm not blaming myself for what happened, but for being so reckless in my decisions. I thought it couldn't happen to me. I was too smart for that, but boy was I wrong.

"A guy I was seeing."

"He's your ex?"

"We didn't date. He was more of a…"

"You slept with him." There's no judgment in his tone. "A hookup."

I'm my harshest critic in this moment. "Yeah. Something bad happened, and I didn't think I'd ever hear from him again."

He tightens his fingers around my wrist. "What does bad mean exactly?"

"I don't want to talk about it, but it was supposed to be handled. He was supposed to be in prison for a long time."

"Prison? Fuck," Hunter hisses.

I nod. I steel my back and force out the story in a short and concise way, needing to tell him what happened without all the gory details. "He attacked Lulu because she and I confronted him about what he did to me. Oliver beat the living crap out of him afterward, but Mark went on trial. He was sentenced to five years, and it hasn't been that long. He's not supposed to be out already."

"We should call the cops," he says.

"No," I beg, finally dragging my gaze away from my lap and to his eyes. "Don't."

"Why?" He strokes his thumb over the skin near my wrist, giving me something else to focus on besides my pounding heart. "You're petrified."

"I need to talk to Lulu and Oliver first. They'll be here soon." I blink a few times, shaking myself out of the haze of fear and rage. "Shit. Harlow."

"I have her," he says with a soft smile. "She's asleep. Well, at least I think she's asleep. I can't see her eyes."

My eyes move from his face to my little niece's. "Yep. She's out like a light."

Hunter shifts and leans back against the cushions. "Come here," he says, motioning for me to get closer to his side.

Without a moment's hesitation, I move into his side,

letting him pull me against him. His body is warm and hard as I sink into him.

"Relax a minute. Mark isn't going to get you. You're safe."

I'm safe. He's not here. I'm safe.

I keep repeating those words to myself, trying to control my breathing and my heart.

It's going to be okay.

I'm going to be okay.

"Close your eyes for a minute," Hunter says, his voice as soothing as his arm that's wrapped around me. "Think of a happy day or place."

"Being with my family in Florida," I say softly.

"Florida sounds good right now."

"Lying on the beach in the sun would be amazing."

"Think of how you felt lying on the beach. Focus on that for a minute. Picture it in your mind."

"Are you secretly a therapist?" My body shakes as Hunter laughs.

"No, but I've done enough of it that I know what to do."

It's not even a little concerning that he's been to therapy. Hell, I did too after what happened because my head wasn't right for a long time.

"Think about the warmth of the sun on your skin…"

He keeps talking, and somewhere along the way, I let myself get too comfortable. I don't know how long passes, but when I open my eyes and turn my head, Hunter's eyes are closed, and he and Harlow are both fast asleep.

My phone buzzes in my lap, and I snatch it up, not wanting them to wake.

Lulu: On our way. Be there in five.

I untangle myself from Hunter's arms, careful not to make the couch dip as I try to stand.

But my butt doesn't make it six inches off the couch before Hunter says, "Hey."

"Sorry," I tell him and let my ass drop back onto the couch.

"For what?"

"I was trying not to wake you."

"I was barely asleep."

The way he was breathing, he was on that beach with me, but I'm not going to argue.

"You have to be tired after working all day. I'm sorry."

"Zoey, babe. Stop apologizing. You didn't do anything wrong."

I blink a few times as I stare at him. "Sorry." I groan, realizing I say that word way too much, especially lately. "Shit."

Hunter's smile makes my heart skip, but in a good way, which is a nice change after the way this night has gone.

"Lulu's almost here."

"We need to talk to her and Oliver."

We?

"I can do it. You can go home and go to bed."

Hunter shakes his head. "I'm not going anywhere."

My gaze dips to Harlow, who's still asleep in his arms. "You're a baby whisperer."

Hunter smiles at me as he lifts his arms, Harlow's legs and arms dangling like she doesn't have a care in the world and she knows she's in a safe spot. "She's a tired little thing."

"Well, she wore herself out with Aunt Zoey, who doesn't know what to do with something so little."

"Babysitting is hard."

"That's no lie," I say, but it hasn't been an issue for him. "I don't think I could do this every day."

"If I did it, anyone can," he says, like somehow when you become a parent, you just know what to do, which I know isn't true.

My phone buzzes again.

Lulu: We're here.

"They're here," I tell him and go to stand, but Hunter grabs my wrist to keep me where I am. "I'll get the door."

"But I…" My words get twisted in my mouth, and I don't know what the right thing to say is. "I can get the door. It's my door."

It's my door? Ugh. What's wrong with me? Between Mark being Mark and Hunter's chivalry, I'm a hot mess and not as smooth as I usually am.

"Not tonight," he says and moves Harlow toward me, wanting me to take her.

He places her in my arms, and thankfully, the kid doesn't wake up. She barely moves. She's oblivious to everything happening around her. She has no idea that she has an aunt who's a train wreck.

I stay on the couch with Harlow in my arms as Hunter goes to the door and opens it, placing himself in the doorway. He glances left and then right, surveying the area.

"Anyone?" I ask, trying to keep the tremble out of my tone.

"Your sister," he says as he waves to her down the hallway. "And Oliver."

"What's wrong?" Lulu asks, her voice carrying down the hallway.

"Nothing. Harlow's asleep," he answers, and if I didn't know better, which I do, I'd believe him.

"Oh. Flowers," Lulu says, and I can see her shadow moving as she starts to bend down.

"Leave them," Hunter tells her, and she freezes.

"What's up?" Oliver asks, his shadow joining Lulu's as she straightens.

"Come in," Hunter tells them and moves his large body out of the doorway.

Lulu rushes into the apartment, her eyes finding me as soon as she's inside. "What happened? Who sent the flowers?"

"Mark," I say, and her entire body goes rigid as she nearly skids to a stop.

Oliver wraps his hands around her shoulders. "Was there a card?"

"Got it," Hunter tells him before I have a chance to open my mouth. Hunter fishes the tiny card out of his pocket and hands it to Oliver.

"What's it say?" Lulu asks, trying to see, but Oliver's too tall for her even in her stiletto boots that are not winter-appropriate.

"Thinking of you," Oliver says in a tone that isn't soft and probably exactly the way Mark meant it.

"Fuck. I'm going to kill him," Lulu says as she snatches the card out of Oliver's hand. She starts to pace, tapping the scrap of paper against her palm. "What the hell happened?"

"He must be out," Oliver replies, swiping his hand down his cheek before scratching his beard.

"I thought they were supposed to notify me when he was released," I tell him, my stomach twisting to the point that I nearly double over.

"I'll call my buddy on the force. We'll get this figured out. You still have a restraining order in place?" Oliver asks me.

Somewhere in the madness, Hunter grabbed my hand, and I missed it. He gives me a light squeeze when I don't answer right away, and my mind shifts back to the present.

"It's still valid."

"I'll stay here with her tonight," Lulu tells Oliver.

"I'll be fine," I say, but no one seems to be paying any attention to me.

"No, sweetheart. I'll do it," Oliver argues as he pulls my sister into his arms and places a kiss on her head.

They're disgustingly cute. Oliver is a catch and one of the best guys I know. He is so much like the men in our family that it was easy for him to slip right in like he'd always been a member.

"I'm staying here with her," Hunter tells them, his eyes meeting mine like he expects me to argue. "You two need to go home and take care of this munchkin."

I'm not going to argue with Hunter. The last thing I want to do tonight is be by myself. What if Mark is lurking in the building, waiting for his chance when I'm finally alone?

Maybe in a few hours when I'm more comfortable and nothing happens, Hunter can go home, and I'll feel safe here by myself.

If I tell him no, my sister or Oliver won't leave, and they need to go back to their place with my sweet little niece.

"Oh Jesus," Lulu mutters, peeling out of Oliver's arms to where Harlow is sleeping in my arms. "I got so wrapped up, and she's so quiet…"

"She's been sleeping for a while," Hunter tells my sister as I give Harlow back to her.

"My girl is a snuggler like her mom."

I tilt my head back and stare at my sister. "Since when have you been a snuggler?"

She lifts her chin and doesn't meet my eyes. "Since Oliver. We do a cuddle pile. The three of us."

I scrunch my nose. "There are things I don't need to know."

"I'll make some calls on the way back to our place and let you know what I find out. If anything happens, call the cops first and me next," Oliver explains to Hunter. "If someone gets in, shoot first and ask questions later."

Hunter looks at Oliver and then at me. "I don't have a gun."

"She does," Oliver says plainly, like we're talking about something less deadly.

"I have a taser too." I give him a timid smile, pretending to be more innocent than I am.

After the attack, I learned to shoot and protect myself because I never wanted to be a victim again. If I have to, which I hope I don't, I will do what I need to do to survive.

"Well, huh," Hunter mutters, looking at me like I'm not the same woman I was a few minutes ago.

"They're locked up," I explain.

"Unlock them. Put them out," Oliver tells me, sounding very much like my father rather than my brother-in-law. "You don't want to be fumbling around for them."

"I've got her. She'll be safe," Hunter says, and for the first time in a long time, I feel like I am.

CHAPTER 14
HUNTER

"I'M SORRY," Zoey says as soon as she closes the door and we're alone.

"Babe," I say, patting the couch cushion next to me. "Come sit."

Her shoulders slump forward, and she walks across the living room like she's about to be grounded. She's so damn cute like this, although there isn't anything cute about the situation. "What?" she asks as soon as she plops down next to me with so much force, my cushion bounces.

I take her hand in mine, wanting and needing her to know a few things. "One, don't apologize again."

"But you're not going to be able to sleep in your bed."

I shake my head. "My bed is shit. It's not a hardship."

The corner of her mouth twitches. "I can be alone. I can protect myself."

"Again, my bed is shit, and I don't want to go."

Her eyebrows rise as her eyes widen. "You really want to stay?"

"I do."

"Okay," she whispers.

"Second, I don't do anything I don't want to do. I offered to stay because I don't want you to be alone tonight. You'll sleep like shit if you're alone."

"You're not wrong," she mutters as her eyes dip to where our hands are interlocked.

"Third, I have a sister, and if this were happening to her, I'd want someone to be there to make her feel safe."

"You're a good guy."

It's nice she thinks so. Most of the time, I think I am too, but there have been moments in my life where I've doubted it.

I have one more thing I need to say. I don't want to, but I can't deny how I'm feeling anymore. I told myself I'd find something wrong or there would be a sign to keep my mouth shut, but it hasn't happened.

Life is short. I've known that for a long time, and every moment I don't say it is a chance wasted.

"And fourth, I want you to be safe because I like you, Zoey."

Her eyebrows rise again as her mouth opens and closes repeatedly like she's glitching. "You…"

"I. Like. You," I repeat, pausing in between each word so her brain can fully process what I said. "I don't want anything to happen to you, and I couldn't go to my place and sleep tonight knowing you were here and panicking. I'm going to stay with you as long as you need until we know you're safe."

"I like you too," she breathes as she gives my hand a squeeze.

A sense of relief washes over me, but my mind instantly slides to the question—now what?

"Now what?" she asks as if she can read my thoughts.

"I don't know," I tell her, being completely honest. "We take things slow."

"I'm good with that. I wasn't looking to fall for anyone."

"You fell for me?" I ask her, staring into her beautiful eyes, wondering how I got so lucky to move next door to her.

Zoey averts her gaze as her cheeks turn pink. "A little bit."

"I fell for you too," I tell her, wanting her to know she's not alone and there's no reason to be embarrassed. "You make it damn hard not to because you're so…"

"Cute?" she asks playfully.

"Beautiful," I correct. "Kids are cute. You're stunning. But more than that, I like your personality."

"Stop." She motions for me to keep going.

I laugh and pull her toward me, tucking her into my side. The mood has shifted. Something I'm thankful for since the evening started as a complete shitshow.

She's more relaxed now. A momentary break in the stress of the flowers and reminders of something that happened to her in the past.

"You ready for bed, or do you want to watch TV?"

"TV," she says, and the words are quickly followed by a yawn. "I'm not ready to go to sleep."

"Put on whatever you want." I shift, getting more comfortable and settling in for the night.

She flips on the television, nestling against me with all her weight. As soon as her head lands on my shoulder, I close my eyes, and before we make it through the starting credits of whatever movie she put on, I drift off to sleep.

————

"Well, you look like shit," Tate says as soon as I walk through the front doors of Inked.

"You're really great with the compliments," I tell her, shrugging off my coat.

She gives me a sugary smile. "Someone was up late. Did it have anything to do with what happened with my cousin last night?"

"Yep." There's no point in lying to her. If she knows something happened to Zoey, she also knows I was there when it happened. "I stayed with her so she wouldn't be alone."

Tate studies me as she taps her pen against the desk. "Is that why you stayed?"

I nod. "She was terrified."

"Mark is an asshole."

"That's what I hear." I stop in front of her, drumming my fingertips against the wood. "Do you think I could have Oliver's number? I want to make sure I'm in the loop."

"Of course," she says, giving me the biggest, most genuine smile. "You need to stay in the loop for sure." She taps her phone screen a few times, and my phone buzzes in my back pocket. "Sent."

"Thanks."

"You like her," Tate says.

"I do."

"Tell her yet?"

"I did."

"Good boy. Kiss yet?"

"None of your business."

Tate pouts when I don't give her the answer she wants. "You're no fun. I'll have to go straight to the source."

"No, we didn't kiss. We're taking it slow."

She groans. "The pace you two are going, you're going to be using a walker by the time you sleep together."

I give her my middle finger before I stalk off, reaching for my phone. I need to touch base with Oliver. I need to know what Mark looks like and as many details as I can get so I know who I'm looking out for and what he's capable of.

Me: Hey. It's Hunter. Can you send me some info on the guy?

It takes less than a minute for him to reply.

Oliver: Here's everything I have on him. If you see him, let me know right away.

The message is followed by a link. When I click it, a folder opens, filled with files that include photos, along with document after document of information on the guy.

I drop down into my chair and start going through the contents. My gut twists at the pictures and the descriptions of all the things the guy did to Zoey and Lulu. I don't know if I could've let Mark keep breathing after what he put the girls through. All I know is that Oliver's a better man than me.

Me: What's the plan?

Oliver: With?

Me: Mark.

Oliver: To put him back in prison.

I raise my eyebrows as I stare at the screen. The man is evolved. Way more than I am, and maybe ever could be.

I spend the next twenty minutes reading over everything Oliver sent. Just when I think it can't get worse, I open the next file and find out it, in fact, can.

I also realize he isn't going to stop. A man like him doesn't send flowers with that message unless he plans to escalate things. We are only at the beginning stages, and hopefully we'll get enough on him to send him back to prison before things spin out of control.

"What's wrong?" Timber asks as he walks by.

I glance up from my phone, my mind reeling. "Just doing some reading."

"I heard about Zoey and that Mark's out of prison," he says.

"Does everyone know everything?" I ask him, but I already know the answer.

"In this family and this shop, the answer is yes. There are no secrets."

I don't want to argue about the difference between secrecy and privacy. I feel like I've been dropped right into a gossip mill, but everything that's been said is the truth. My sister and I share everything too, but we are as far as the details are passed. The Gallo family and their ethos is bigger than I could've comprehended before stepping into their world, but it is finally starting to become clear.

"Are they always this open and honest?"

"Yep, and sometimes it's too much," he replies with his face buried in his phone as he sits down at his station across from me. "But you get used to it."

"Do you, though?" I ask, not believing it for a minute.

"You don't really have a choice."

I sit on his answer, letting that hard truth settle deep in my gut. I didn't dislike it.

"But they're also not a judgmental bunch either, which makes the sharing all your life details easier to stomach. My family, on the other hand, is vicious. They more resemble a pack of rabid dogs than a sweet and loving group of people."

"Sucks," I tell him, but right now, I'd take rabid dogs over dead parents any day of the week. At least they would be alive and breathing.

"Yeah." He glances up, staring at me. "You into Zoey, or are you sick of Tate bothering you about her?"

"I'm into her," I tell him honestly, finding it's the only way to go around all of them.

"Cool," he mutters. "She's a good one."

"I think so," I tell him, making myself busy.

"Keep her safe. Mark's a sicko."

"That's the plan," I say, hoping the problem ends before it really has a chance to begin.

"He's a wackadoodle."

I chuckle softly. Chicago, man. The words they use are so different from anything I heard in my hometown. Besides in movies, no one in my real life has ever called another human being a wackadoodle before now. "Men like him are cowards."

"She has to be scared."

"She's good at pretending she's not, but I made sure she was okay before I came here. Lulu stopped over as I was leaving."

"You stayed with her last night?" he asks.

"Yeah."

"You staying with her tonight?"

"Yes," I say without a moment's hesitation. "I'll stay as long as I need to for her to feel safe." Even if that means forever.

CHAPTER 15
ZOEY

I LOVE MY SISTER, but sometimes she's over the top. Well, maybe more than sometimes. She's been a drama queen since the day I was born—and well before that, from what my mother says. But sometimes it's even a bit much for me, which is saying something because I'm a drama llama too.

"Another cup?" I ask her when she finally takes a breath.

She's been yammering about Mark for over an hour. She's venting everything I'm feeling and going over our tragic past with him, which we were luckily able to escape for years while he was behind bars.

"I really shouldn't," she replies, but she lifts her cup, wanting a top off.

The girl is a bigger caffeine addict than me. I wasn't sure she was going to survive not having any during her pregnancy, but the moment the baby came out, she downed coffee like it was the best thing in the world.

"How did things go with Hunter last night?" Zoey

takes a sip and closes her eyes, savoring the mid-level coffee like it's a life-changing experience. "Did he stay all night?"

"We fell asleep on the couch watching a movie."

She raises a perfectly styled eyebrow. "Opposite sides of the couch or the same?"

I set my mug down on the counter and lean forward on my elbows. "We may have snuggled."

Her other eyebrow lifts, making a matching set. "You cuddled?" she gasps and covers her mouth. "Zoey's a cuddler."

"It was an extreme situation." I pick at a dried food spot on the granite. I hate this counter. It is impossible to find every bit of dirt unless you get down to eye level with the stone. "I wasn't myself."

"When I walked into your apartment and you two were taking care of Harlow, I have to say the entire scene made my heart skip a little."

"Don't get ahead of yourself, sissy."

She waves me off with her free hand, careful not to spill any of her coffee. "I'm not, but I know you like him, and he likes you."

"I know. We told each other last night after he wouldn't leave," I confess. She'll find out eventually, and honestly, I need to tell someone. And there's no better person than her. She knows all my secrets, and I know hers.

"You told each other?" She's so interested in the answer, she places her coffee on the counter and gives me her undivided attention. "Like, *told each other*, told each other?"

"Uh…" I stammer, staring at her. "How else do you say it? He said he liked me." I pause and think about how the conversation happened. "He said it twice, and then I told him how I felt too."

"That's huge, Zo," she says softly and reaches out to touch my hand. "I'm proud and excited for you."

"It could go nowhere."

"Is he staying again tonight?"

I nod. "He said he'll walk me home from work tonight and stay. He said he doesn't want me to be alone until we have the Mark situation under control."

Lulu sighs. "Oliver's losing it over this entire clusterfuck. He wouldn't let me come over here alone. He dropped me off and took Harlow to do a job before they swing back to get me. I'm not interested in having a babysitter again."

"I'm sorry. It's all my fault."

"Don't," she snaps, tightening her hand on mine. "Don't apologize for him. You're not at fault for Mark being a freaking lunatic."

"Okay," I breathe. "You're right."

"Now, tell me more about Hunter."

"What about him?" I grab my coffee again, done with all the touchy-feely stuff.

"Is he a good kisser?"

"We haven't kissed."

Her mouth hangs open like I just announced something shocking. "You're kidding me."

I shake my head. "We're taking things slow."

"I'm going to have gray hair by the time you two act on your feelings."

I roll my eyes. "He's going through a lot too."

"Like what?"

"He moved here earlier than he planned to be closer to his daughter while his ex goes through cancer treatment."

Lulu clutches her chest. "Oh my God. That's so sad. The little girl has to be so scared."

"They're doing a good job of keeping her in the loop and also keeping her calm."

"I don't know if I could do that."

"Who could in our family?" I ask and crack a smile.

"The sky is always falling with us." She shrugs. "Dad would've kept us calm, though."

"Lucio has been trying to keep us calm his entire life —and often without success," I tell her.

"You better not let him hear you call him Lucio."

We giggle, sounding so much like we did when we were little girls and up to no good.

"I'm too old to ground," I say as I push away from the counter to dump what's left of my coffee in the sink.

"That's a travesty."

"What?" I ask her without looking over my shoulder.

"Wasting coffee."

"You should walk around with an IV of it all day."

"If I could, I would. Thankfully, Harlow is sleeping through the night now. I felt like the walking dead for a while."

"I couldn't do it."

"Yes, you could. Someday, you will."

"I'm never having kids, Lu."

She gasps and grabs the counter like she is about to fall off her stool. "What? You can't be serious. Why would you say that?"

I turn around, leaning back against the counter in front of the sink. "I was there when Harlow was born."

"I remember. Vaguely, but I remember. Parts of that day were a blur."

"Not a blur for me," I mutter under my breath. "Childbirth is horrifying. I promised myself as I watched my beautiful niece being born that I was never putting myself through that."

Lulu slaps her hand over her eyes and groans. "You're an idiot."

"I am not."

"Sure, it hurts, but it's worth it. I barely remember the pain from that day, and the epidural kicked ass. You have more than one tattoo, don't you?"

"A tattoo is nothing like your body splitting open as a human being tears its way out."

"I didn't split open. Hell, I didn't even tear. Not even a little," she says.

I don't know if she thinks her answer is going to make me change my mind, but it doesn't. I will never— and I mean never—get the visuals from that day out of my head.

I cover my mouth, holding back the bile that's rising in my throat just thinking about that being a possibility. "You can talk until you're blue in the face about how beautiful it is, but my answer will always be the same… never happening."

"Whatever," she mumbles, waving me off like I'm

being silly. "Well, the man already has one kid. I'm sure he'll want another."

I stare at her, dumbfounded. In her head, she already has us married off and starting a family. I've known the guy only a few weeks at most, and we haven't even kissed. She's jumping way ahead of herself—hell, way ahead of me.

"He has one. That's enough."

Lulu's about to say something, but her phone buzzes. "Oliver's back. I have to go. Need a ride to the bar?" She slides off the stool and takes a final sip of her coffee.

"No. Mason's coming to get me," I tell her.

I know my sister hates feeling like she has a babysitter, but now, she's doing it to me. I'm surprised my parents aren't at my door to watch over me until Mark is out of the picture.

She gives me a bear hug and a kiss on the cheek. "You stay safe."

"You too," I tell her, hoping Mark's attention stays on me and away from her.

When Lulu opens the door, Mason's already standing in the hallway.

I roll my eyes and sigh. A girl can't get a little alone time when there's a stalker on the loose. I'm already over the entire situation, and it's only just begun.

"Oh good. You're here," Lulu says to him before she pops up on her tiptoes and gives Mason a kiss on the cheek. "Keep an eye on her."

"Keep an eye out for him. I don't need any more eyes on me," I correct her.

"I got it," Mason tells her as she heads toward the elevator to her husband and baby waiting in the truck outside.

Mason stalks into the apartment and kicks off his shoes. "I'm exhausted," he says as he makes his way to my couch and collapses. "I'm ready to go back to bed."

"Close your eyes. I need some time to get ready before we head to the bar."

"Can I have like thirty minutes?"

I glance down at my watch and realize he's way earlier than he needs to be. "You can have forty-five."

"Thank God," he breathes and closes his eyes.

Old me would've immediately started plotting how to slip out of the apartment without him waking up, but I'm not a teenager anymore and I have more sense...at least sometimes I do.

"I'm going to hop in the shower and get ready. I'll wake you when I'm ready."

Exactly forty-five minutes later, I'm finished. I didn't wash my hair today because I didn't have the time and opted for an updo to make my locks a little more manageable. I put on a thick sweater with a long-sleeved shirt underneath for when I become over-heated at the bar, which happens often in the winter. My jeans are snug this morning, but I always get bloated when I am stressed out. And to feel a little more empowered, I decide to wear my black combat boots instead of my knee-length boots with stiletto heels.

"Mason." I bump the edge of the couch with my hip. "I'm ready."

He stretches and groans, taking up the entire couch with his large frame. "That was fast."

"I could start the shift without you, and you can meet me there."

"No," he says as he pulls his body upward to a sitting position. "Can't do that."

Of course not. He's been tasked with my protection, and if he didn't walk me to work, my mother would chew his ear off.

"Then let's go," I say, grabbing my coat from the hook near the door, ready to get the day started.

———

The bar is busier than we expected. That's become a common occurrence lately because the only other restaurant on the block was turned into an upscale salon. I can't complain, though, because we are making more money than we ever have since the place was opened more than fifty years ago.

As I deliver a pizza to a table of women having cocktails after work, the door to the bar opens and Hunter walks in.

"Can I get you anything else?" I ask the women as I set the pizza down on their table.

"No. We're good. We'll need another round in a bit," the one woman with blond hair says as she hands out the plates I left earlier.

"I'll be back soon," I promise them as my eyes track Hunter stalking through the dining room to sit on an open stool at the bar.

Mason greets him, shaking hands and saying something that I can't make out because it's too loud in here and I've always been shit at reading lips.

I make my way behind the bar, taking a few requests for more beers from some regulars.

"Hey," I say to Hunter as soon as I'm close enough for him to hear. "What's up?" I reach into the cooler, grabbing a couple drinks.

"I have a break between customers, and I'm hungry." His eyes rake over me, taking in my outfit. "I love the sweater."

"Thank you," I tell him, popping the caps off the beer bottles before I deliver them. "Burger?"

"With cheese and to go."

"Got it," I say before leaving him for a minute to deliver the drinks and ring in his order.

When I glance his way, he's leaning forward, noticing my boots. "Combat?"

"Stilettos and ice don't mix."

He runs his fingertips down his beard, scratching. "Smart."

"You need lotion." I lift my chin toward him. "Skin gets too dry with this weather."

"Lotion my beard?"

"Or some balm. I may have some at my place you could use. The wind is only going to get worse, and you're only going to get itchier."

"I can't imagine that," he says as his hand switches sides. His eyes close, and his lips part as he hits one spot. I've been there. Sometimes there's nothing more satisfying than scratching an itch.

"Trust me. My skin is as dry as the Sahara by the time January rolls around."

"I know nothing about this stuff," he tells me.

But I already knew that. We haven't touched much, but the few times our hands have brushed, his were dry. Not his hands, but his knuckles. And with all the tattooing, I know he is washing his hands dozens of times every single day, and that only makes things worse.

"Are you doing okay?" he asks when I lean over the bar in front of him, letting my back take a break and stretch.

"I'm great. Why?"

His gaze moves across my face, studying me in a way that makes me squirm. "You're great?"

"Don't I look great?" I'm being argumentative. I know I am, but I'm not breakable or ready to lose my marbles because I received flowers from the jackass.

"You look better than great."

"Good man," I praise him.

"Should we bring home a pizza tonight?" he asks me.

My belly flips a little. Home. The way those words slid off his tongue sounds like we live together, and we've had this conversation all the time.

"Pizza would be great. You think you can stay awake for the entire movie this time?" I smirk at him, loving that I'm able to tease him without him getting all bent out of shape.

"Did you make it much further than me?"

"I watched the whole thing," I lie.

He stares at me, and I know he wants to call me on

my bullshit. I can see it in his eyes. Did I watch the whole movie? Absolutely not. Would I admit that I fell asleep shortly after him? Also a big no.

"I'll stay awake tonight."

"We'll see. You want to make a bet?"

Hunter rubs his hands together. "Are you talking money?"

"Foot rubs," I tell him, because I don't need any more money, but foot rubs are always appreciated. When I get off work after being on my feet for hours, there's nothing more delicious than someone rubbing the soreness away.

"I'm down with that," he says with a nod as his lips curve into a smile and his blue eyes sparkle.

"I could stay up all night if it means someone will rub my feet."

"Baby, I'll rub your feet without you having to lose a bet."

My eyebrows rise at his admission. "Did I tell you that I like you?" I tease, but man, I *like him* like him, and the more I get to know him and the more time I spend with him, the deeper I seem to be falling.

"Burger," Mason says, breaking our playful banter and the moment by weaseling his way between me and the bar. He looks at Hunter and then me as he sets down the to-go bag on the bar. "Was I interrupting something?"

"Aren't you always?" I ask.

The man has always had a knack for killing moments since he was a little boy. It's as if he was born with the gift of mood-killing and hasn't been able to grow out of it. I'm not sure if it's because he doesn't pay attention to anyone except himself or he just doesn't care.

"I'll be back after closing to get you," Hunter says, grabbing the bag with his burger inside.

"I'll be waiting for that foot rub," I tell him with a wink before he stalks out of the bar, his bag in hand.

"Ick," Mason mumbles. "That's gross."

"You better start liking feet if you want a wife. There's nothing better than having a man rub my feet."

"I don't mind feet, but your feet are…" His voice trails off as he grimaces.

I hip check him so hard his body jolts. "You're a jerk. I have pretty feet."

"They look like mine," he says, and my eyes widen.

"I don't have your ugly claws."

"You do," he says and glances down. "Yours are just painted."

Cousins suck sometimes, and I wouldn't trade him for the world, but there is no way in hell I have his toes or feet.

CHAPTER 16
HUNTER

I SHAKE OUT MY HANDS, pacing outside the Hook & Hustle.

Why am I so nervous?

I already told her that I liked her, sounding very much like we were in high school and I had a crush on her.

What could have my heart racing and my palms sweating?

I promised myself I wouldn't get involved with anyone until Natalie was in the clear. But damn it, Zoey made it impossible for me not to like her.

And maybe my sister was right. How long was I going to put off my chance at happiness? I'm not getting any younger, and every year passes a little faster than the one before.

"What are you doing?" Zoey asks from the doorway of the bar, and I nearly jump out of my skin.

"Shit." I clutch my chest as I turn around to find her staring at me. "Sorry. I wanted to give you some time."

"In this freezing-ass cold?" She lifts an eyebrow, calling my bluff or my insanity.

"I was hot," I lie, doing my best not to shiver as a gust of cold air hits me square in the face.

Zoey laughs and motions for me to come inside. "Get in here before you get frostbite. I'm almost ready to go."

The bar is still open, and the place is packed. There's only one seat open around the bar, and every table is filled. "Are you giving shit away?" I ask as I follow her.

"You'd think so," she says over her shoulder when a group at one table starts to yell back and forth but not in a way that's alarming to anyone in the place.

I slide onto the open stool to wait for her, and a beer is in front of me a few seconds later. When I look up, Mason's standing before me on the other side of the bar. "Figured you'd need one."

"More than you know," I tell him.

Work was rough tonight. I had two women with horrific stories, and both wanted Medusa tattoos. There wasn't much talking, but the little they did was impactful and ripped out my heart. I was honored that they picked me to do their ink, and hopefully it gives them some of their power back.

"So, when's Lizzy coming to town?" Mason asks, rolling a toothpick around his mouth with his tongue.

"You're going to choke on that," I tell him, pointing at the wooden stick that could very easily slide down his throat and get lodged there with no hope of a rescue without a trip to the hospital.

He pulls the toothpick from between his lips and slides it behind his ear. "So…Lizzy."

"This weekend." I take a sip of my beer, ignoring the cold as it slides down my throat to my stomach. I could've gone for something hot on a cold night like this, but the alcohol is needed more than the warmth.

His face morphs into an easy, satisfied smile. "I'll have to drop by and say hello."

"I'm sure she'd like that," I say, throwing him a bone. He's not a bad guy. I mean, he can't be if he's Zoey and Lulu's cousin. They don't seem to put up with too much shit, and if he were an asshole, I have no doubt they'd set his ass straight in a hurry.

His eyebrows rise as his eyes widen. "Really? You're okay with that?"

"Sure," I say around the rim of my beer.

Lizzy put up with about as much bullshit as Lulu and Zoey, so I know she could handle her own with Mason. It doesn't hurt that she likes the guy, and although I am her older brother, she is a full-grown woman and doesn't need my protection from everyone.

"It's Zoey's Christmas party this weekend. Maybe she'll come and we can hang out there."

I'd completely forgotten about her party. Lulu invited me when I first moved in, but it had slipped my mind. "We'll both be there," I tell him with a dip of my chin.

"It may be the first year I'm looking forward to it, then."

Zoey comes up behind him and asks, "Looking forward to what?"

Mason jolts at the sound of her voice, but he quickly rebounds. "Your Christmas party. Although it's not Christmas yet."

"I like to do it before everyone gets too busy. Early December is perfect," she replies.

"I like it," I say.

"You like everything she says," Mason states with an added eye roll. "Suck up."

I can't argue with him. I won't disagree with Zoey about anything, especially at this point in our relationship.

I sober, my stomach dropping.

Is that what we were in? Have we hit that stage yet? Does saying that you like someone mean you are *together* together? I haven't dated in over a decade, and I have no clue how shit works now.

"You okay?" Zoey asks, touching my hand from across the bar. "Your face drained of all its color."

"Yeah," I say, finding my voice after clearing my throat. "I'm fine. Good. Great, really."

I am fine too. Better than fine. For the first time in a long time, I feel like there is a world of possibilities in front of me. A new town. New job. And maybe even a new girl.

She stares at me for a few seconds, unconvinced of my answer, before she turns to Mason. "You're okay with me going now?"

"Yeah. You two get out of here," he says. "There're enough workers here tonight to help me close up."

Zoey lifts on her toes and kisses her cousin's cheek.

"You don't have to tell me twice," she says before skipping away to grab her stuff.

I know that's my cue. We're headed home, which means a walk in the freezing cold. I down what's left of my beer, needing the alcohol to give me a false sense of warmth.

Before I moved here, people warned me about the frigid cold. I thought they were yanking my chain, but in the few weeks I've been here and experienced the start of winter, I've learned they weren't being dramatic.

"I'm ready," Zoey says, coming out of the back room with her coat half on and carrying our pizza. "Let's go before he changes his mind."

I place my hand on the small of her back, ushering her toward the door, although she doesn't need the extra push. As soon as we're outside, she twirls around with her face toward the sky. The snowflakes land on her cheeks and instantly melt.

"I feel like I'm skipping school," she says with her arms wide, looking every bit like a little kid finally gaining their first taste of true freedom.

"I like this side of you," I tell her, unable to wipe the smile off my face.

She stops, turns to me, and closes the space between us in a few short steps. "You like all sides of me," she says, grabbing my coat and hauling me flat against her. "Don't you?"

I stare into her eyes, my heart racing as I slide my arms around her, holding her close against me. Her breath is the only warmth around us.

"I want to kiss you," I tell her, choosing honesty instead of questioning if this is the right time or place.

"Then do it," she whispers before her gaze dips to my mouth as she licks her lips.

I don't overthink it as I lean forward, taking her mouth with mine. The kiss isn't soft or gentle as our lips meet, sending a bolt of electricity through my body that I've never felt before. The sounds of the city melt away around us, creating a bubble where only we exist.

She slides her fingers through the hair at the back of my head and I groan at the contact, but my knees go weak when she rakes her nails downward along the same path.

I deepen the kiss like a starved man, wanting to taste, needing this connection more than I need to breathe.

Zoey kisses me back with as much ferocity and hunger as I do her. I slip my hands under her jacket, finding her warm skin. She jolts at the cold but doesn't pull away as I drop my hands to her ass, not wanting her to freeze.

Giggles sound around us, bringing us back to reality. She pulls away first, her eyes soft and lips puffy. I blink a few times, trying to clear my mind from the haze of lust that's taken over.

"That was hot," a woman says, barely able to stand upright if her friend weren't holding her.

"Sooo hot," the friend tells her as they wobble down the sidewalk in a zigzag pattern, clearly drunk.

Zoey smirks as she looks at me. "It was," she says,

agreeing with the two women who interrupted the most amazing kiss I may have had in my entire life.

I hold out a hand, wanting to get out of here. "Home?" I ask.

She slides her warm palm into mine and nods. "And more kissing."

"Perfect," I say, closing my fingers around hers.

Before I take a step, a crack rings through the air, and I'm thrown backward like I've been struck by lightning.

I fall to the ground, my head tilting to the side to see a man running down the street, glancing over his shoulder with terror in his eyes.

"Hunter!" Zoey screams as her warm hands touch my face.

"What..." I try to say, but speaking is a struggle.

"Stay still!" she yells.

I want to tell her she doesn't have to scream. I can hear her fine, but the pain lancing through my chest makes it too hard to force out words.

The world around me goes fuzzy. The streetlights and neon signs start to fade, and I close my eyes, focusing on my struggling breaths and the sound of Zoey's voice.

CHAPTER 17
ZOEY

MY HANDS SHAKE as I pat my pockets, trying to find my damn phone. I pull it out, barely able to dial 9-1-1 as Hunter lies on the ground in front of me.

Blood has covered his coat, and the spot is getting bigger with each passing second.

Breathe, Zoey.

When the dispatcher finally picks up, I rattle off where we are and what happened before I let the phone drop to the sidewalk next to him.

"Hunter," I say again, touching his cheeks, trying to get him to open his eyes.

"Fuck," a voice hisses from behind me before the person touches my shoulders. "What happened, Zo?" It's Mason standing over me, but I'm too panicked to feel any type of consolation from his presence.

"I don't know. He's bleeding," I say, sounding like an idiot, but I've never heard a sound like that before to know what's going on.

My mind is spinning, working a thousand miles a second.

"Was he shot?" my cousin asks, and the pieces slide into place.

"Yes," I tell him. "Hunter." I cradle his face in my hands, watching his chest move up and down.

He's still alive.

"I'll call 9-1-1."

I don't turn around, giving my full attention to the man in front of me, who I was kissing only a moment before. "I already did."

Mason moves to Hunter's other side, grabbing his wrist. "He has a pulse."

"Thanks, McDreamy."

"What?" he asks, still clutching Hunter's arm.

"Nothing," I say, hating that I'm being a bitch when my cousin's trying to help.

A crowd has gathered around us now. Everyone from inside the bar has come out to see what's going on.

"He can't die," I whisper. "He can't die."

I repeat those words to myself over and over, trying to convince myself that it's not possible. It can't end like this. Not before we've had a chance to truly begin.

We kissed. A magical kiss. The best one I've ever had, and for it all to end like this would be...darkly tragic. If we hadn't stopped, if I hadn't told him to kiss me, we'd be on our way home right now, and none of this would've happened.

"He won't die," Mason says. "He's tough."

He may be tough, but that doesn't matter when it comes to a bullet. He could be the strongest guy in the world, and a gunshot could end him in the blink of an eye.

"Did you see who did it?" Mason asks.

I shake my head as the memory of that split second plays on repeat in my mind.

I heard the noise, saw Hunter jolt with his eyes wide, before he toppled backward like I'd pushed him over. I didn't have a moment to look around or do anything before he was on the ground with blood covering the front of him.

Before Mason has a chance to ask anything else, the sirens echo off the old buildings on the street, and a small sliver of me feels a little relief. He has a chance.

"Hunter," I say again, but he doesn't open his eyes. "The ambulance is here. You're going to be okay."

"He will be," my cousin says.

I glance around, staring at all the blood, and wonder if I'm lying to myself. How does someone survive when it looks like every drop that could possibly have been inside them is outside their body?

"Ma'am, step away. We've got this," a man says, pulling me gently away from Hunter's side.

The paramedics are here, and they waste no time in getting to work on Hunter as Mason helps me to my feet and keeps his arm around me.

"Who would do this?" I whisper, asking myself the question because no one has an answer. I'm shaking in Mason's embrace, and he does his best to make me feel safe.

"Sir. Ma'am," a uniformed officer says, tipping his head to us both. "Did either of you see who did this?"

I shake my head, unable to tear my gaze away from Hunter's motionless body. The paramedics are working fast, taking vitals and doing other stuff I don't understand.

"I was inside, but she didn't see anything," Mason replies for us.

"We'll have to pull the security footage from some of the buildings," the officer says.

"We have cameras. I own the bar with my cousin," Mason replies.

"That would be helpful and the quickest route to finding the person who's responsible."

The cameras. I totally forgot we installed them five years ago after we convinced everyone they were a necessary expense. The inside and outside of the bar have a state-of-the-art system and over ten different camera angles to keep us safe, along with our customers.

"Will you be okay?" Mason asks me.

"Go," I tell him. "I'm going with Hunter."

I won't leave his side. I can't.

The paramedics put Hunter on the stretcher, and I step forward, my feet moving without much thought. I follow them to the ambulance and prepare myself for whatever I see inside.

"Ma'am," the paramedic says, and before he has a chance to add anything, I make my feelings known.

"I'm going with him."

He nods, his lips tight. "Just give us room to work."

I climb in after they load Hunter, and then the paramedic gets in with me. The back is filled with a lot of machines and supplies, and as soon as the front door slams, we're moving. I hold on to something, hoping I'm not going to break an expensive piece of equipment, but it's either me or whatever the hell it is at this point.

It all passes in a blur as we hit pothole after pothole, jostling everyone inside. I don't even know how the paramedic is able to get an IV into Hunter with all the bumps, but he does and makes it look effortless too.

"Are you next of kin?" the man asks me, but I'm too zoned out, unable to take my eyes off Hunter. "Ma'am."

"No," I whisper, and my stomach sinks.

They need someone who's legally able to speak for him, and that person isn't me.

"Do you know how to contact his next of kin?" He doesn't look at me as he checks Hunter's wound, covering it with some gauze and applying pressure.

"I could call his sister," I say, but it's as if I'm having an out-of-body experience. It's like I'm floating above us, watching everything unfold instead of actively participating.

"Call her. The hospital will need to talk to her."

"His phone," I tell the man and swallow, knowing I can't get it myself. "It's in his pocket."

"You know his code?" the paramedic asks as he reaches into Hunter's coat pocket and gets his cell phone.

"No."

He lifts Hunter's hand and places his thumb on the screen, unlocking it. "Here you go."

"Thanks," I say, but I'm a little shocked at how easy

it was for him to do that. In my state of mind, I never would've thought to do that.

I go to Hunter's contacts and find Lizzy's number. My finger hovers over the screen as I take a deep breath. How do I tell her? She's going to lose it.

I hit call, and it's already ringing by the time I place the phone on speaker.

"What's up, big brother?" Her voice is full of cheer, and every bit of me wants to hang up and not ruin her night.

"Hey, Lizzy. It's Zoey." My voice is quiet, like it's going to soften the blow somehow.

"What's wrong?" she says quickly. "Where's Hunter?"

"Don't panic," I say. It's what everyone always says, and it's the dumbest thing in the world because it has the opposite effect. "He was shot, but he's alive."

She gasps. "He was what?"

"He was shot, but he's alive." I make sure to repeat that part of my previous statement. "I'm in the ambulance with him and we're on the way to the hospital, but they're going to need to talk to you since you're next of kin."

There's a ton of noise on her end of the line. I imagine she's packing things or just in a general panic, unsure of what to do. "Is he awake?"

"Not at the moment."

"I'm coming. I'll find a flight and be there."

"Ma'am, this is Tom. I'm the paramedic. We'll need you to be available to take a call from the hospital.

They're going to need permission to treat him, depending on the severity of the bullet wound."

"Of course. I'll keep my phone on. I won't get on a plane until I hear from them. Which hospital?"

The paramedic rattles off the details to her.

"I'll stay with him, Lizzy, and text you what's going on. How long is the flight?"

"Forty-five minutes. Hopefully there's a flight leaving soon. I could be there in a few hours."

"Okay," I say. "I'll keep you posted."

"Fuck. This is crazy."

"I know. I'm so sorry."

"Don't say you're sorry. He's not dead," she says.

"He's not. He's not going to die," I tell her, but I'm not sure I completely believe the words I'm saying.

"I'll be there soon. Bye," she says.

"Bye," I reply, but I think she's already disconnected the call.

I take a moment and enter her contact information into my phone, because as soon as his screen turns off, it'll lock again.

The sirens turn off, and the ambulance starts to slow. "We're pulling in. Things are about to get busy. Stay out of the way and follow."

"Got it." I brace myself as we come to a halt.

He made it here. He's still breathing, even though the paramedic has changed the gauze a few times because it's become saturated.

The doors open, and numerous people are almost yelling at one another, calling out information as they whisk Hunter and the gurney out of the back of the ambulance. They're running through the emergency room doors by the time I jump down from the back of the ambulance. I do my best, barely able to keep up with them and staying out of their way the best I can.

"Ma'am," a nurse says, or at least I think she's a nurse. "Why don't you wait outside the room? I could use some information."

My eyes are on Hunter as they cut off his clothes, including his blood-soaked sweater. "Okay," I whisper as she takes my hand, guiding me out of the emergency room trauma bay.

I follow her down the hallway to a private room with a couch and low lights. It's soothing—or at least as calming as a room can be for people in my circumstances.

"Would you like some water?" she asks as I sit down.

My leg shakes, and I cover my knee with my hand, trying to stop it from moving. If I could pace a path across this small room, I would, but there's too much furniture in relation to the square footage.

"Name?"

"Zoey Gallo."

The woman smiles. "Hi, Zoey. I need his name."

"Of course. Shit. Sorry. Hunter."

"Hunter what?"

I stare at her, and she stares back.

Damn. Do I know his last name? My mind can't process much, and I'm not sure if I ever heard his last name. If I came off stupid after telling her my name, it's about to get worse. "I don't know."

"Do you know his date of birth or age?"

"Um, thirties," I say, wincing. "We only met a few weeks ago, and he's my neighbor. I didn't get a ton of details."

"It's okay. Do you know if his next of kin has been contacted?"

I nod. "I called his sister. I have her number."

"May I have it?"

I pull out my phone and find Lizzy's number, reading each digit to her twice. "She's on her way here from Ohio."

"I'll make the doctors aware so they can call her right away."

"Thank you."

The door to the small room opens, and a woman walks in. "Hello. I'm Dr. Katz. Are you here with Hunter?"

I nod again, unable to find my words.

"He has internal bleeding from the gunshot wound. He needs emergency surgery to stop the bleeding. Are you next of kin?"

Damn. I never knew it was that important that you have a next of kin. Who is mine? Lulu or my parents? I'm not sure, but I hope it's Lulu because I wouldn't want my parents to make any decisions if they are ever in a panic like I am now.

"No. His sister, and she's on her way from out of state."

"Here," the woman I had been talking to says, handing Dr. Katz a slip of paper with Lizzy's contact information.

"Will he live?" I ask, staring up at her as I wait for the floor to fall out from under me.

"We'll know more once we're in surgery. He's lost a lot of blood."

She gave an answer, but not one to my question.

She holds up the slip of paper. "I need to make this call."

I nod again, dropping my head to stare at my hands in my lap.

He may die. Fuck. He may *really* die.

On the ambulance ride, I felt like he was getting help and that he'd pull through. The same feeling stayed with me when we got here and an entire team started to evaluate and work on him. But after the nonanswer from Dr. Katz, I'm not so sure.

The nurse stands up from the chair next to me. "I'll be back soon to check in on you."

"Can I go out to the waiting room?" I ask.

I can't stay in here by myself, sitting in silence. I'll have a bigger panic attack than I already am, and I'll end up in a bed down the hall, which is the last thing anyone needs in this situation.

"Sure. We'll come out when we know more. He'll be in surgery for a few hours at least."

"Hopefully his sister will be here by then," I tell her as I stand.

"Let us know when she is. The waiting room is down the hall on your right."

I give her a small smile. One I'm not feeling at all, but I've been programmed to smile even when it's not appropriate or heartfelt.

I keep my eyes trained on the hallway as I pass by room after room of patients in various stages of pain and injury. It's overwhelming. I don't know how anyone can work in an emergency room and keep their sanity or happiness after seeing what they see.

When I step into the waiting room, Mason is there, along with my parents, Tate, Lulu, and Oliver.

I run to my dad and collapse in his arms. I mumble out a few words, none of them making sense through the tears, and completely fall apart.

CHAPTER 18
ZOEY

I OPEN my eyes and blink a few times, wondering if I am imagining things or caught in a bad dream.

Lizzy sits across from me with Mason's arm slung around her. She's blotting her cheeks with a tissue as my cousin speaks softly to her.

Shit. I didn't dream Hunter had been shot. No. He really was shot, and we are sitting in the waiting room.

My heart rate skyrockets as the realization washes over me. I bolt upright in the chair, and my father squeezes my hand.

"It's okay, sweetheart," he says as Lizzy's gaze finds mine.

"Is he…" I can't finish the sentence. "How long was I out?"

"A couple hours," my dad replies. "The surgeon hasn't come out, but we expect to hear something soon. Lizzy's spoken to the nurses."

A couple hours? How could I pass out at a time like this?

I push off the chair and rush to Lizzy. She leaps up and embraces me as if she needs the connection as much as I do.

"I'm sorry. I'm so, so sorry," I tell her as I hug her tightly.

"Don't apologize, Zo," she replies and sniffles. "He's going to be okay. He's a tough one. I know my brother, and he isn't going out like this. He has too much to fight for."

"Oh my God. Amira," I whisper, a new set of tears flooding my eyes.

"And you," she states, like I'm an idiot for not including myself in his reasons to stay alive.

I pull back and stare into her eyes. "It's my fault."

She shakes her head, mustering a small smile. "It's not your fault."

I babble on about how he had to walk me home and what happened after we left the bar. I recount the entire series of events from the twirling to the kiss.

Lizzy listens to every word as she grips my arm. "That doesn't make it your fault. The only person at fault is the person who shot him."

Suddenly, I remember Mason being there when Hunter was loaded into the ambulance. The officer who was asking us questions. My cousin telling him about the security cameras.

I peer down at Mason as he watches us. "Did you see anything on the security footage?"

Mason nods, his lips turning down at the corners. "The cops have it now."

"Was it an accident?" Lizzy asks as she sits down.

This time, Mason shakes his head, his face draining of color. "It was Mark."

My body goes numb, and I stagger backward like someone sucker-punched me in the gut. All the air leaves my body, and I'm instantly light-headed.

It is my fault. It is, and nobody can tell me any different. First, Mark attacked Lulu because of me—and now Hunter. I am the root cause of the people I care about being hurt by a vicious and vindictive man.

"They're out looking for him," Dad adds from behind me. "They'll get him."

"Honey," Mom says, coming up behind me and grabbing my shoulders. "Why don't you sit down?"

I sway as she helps me back to my chair at my father's side. "It's my fault," I whisper, and tears stream down my cheeks in a torrent. I'm in too much shock to stop them as they plop onto my coat like raindrops during a thunderstorm.

A nurse approaches us and stops at the end of our row. "Hunter's family?"

Lizzy nods. "I'm his sister."

"We're his family," Dad answers without skipping a beat. "How is he?"

"He's doing well. They've been able to stop the bleeding and are just making sure everything is good before closing him up. The doctor will be out to talk to you as soon as surgery is over."

"Does that mean he'll live?" Lizzy asks, sitting up stiff as a board at my cousin's side.

Mason reaches over, taking Lizzy's hand in his. I clock the movement even though this still feels like a bad dream. I don't know if I've ever seen this loving, caring side of my cousin with anyone except family. It's sweet and endearing, reminding me very much of my uncle Angelo.

"He's alive and fighting is all I can say. The doctor will be out soon." The woman gives us a stiff smile with sorrowful eyes before she turns around and leaves.

A sense of relief washes over me. He's alive, and he is fighting. I never doubted that. Everyone fights to live, but at some point, the ability to stay on this earth is taken from them. Whether it be the skill of the doctor or some greater force, we don't always get to control whether we continue to breathe.

"Oh, thank God," Lizzy says as Mason pulls her back down into her chair. She curls into him, a fresh wave of sobs overtaking her.

She's not the only one in tears. Every single woman sitting with us is crying, while my dad and Mason hold their shit together as if it's their duty to make sure they're strong for us.

I stare straight ahead, unable to process much of anything as people come and go from the surgical waiting room and life carries on around us like it's any average day.

But it's not average.

Life hasn't gone on for me or for Hunter.

He was shot, and I was the target.

"Hey," Dad says, pulling me under his shoulder. "Get out of your own head."

"I can't."

"He's going to be okay, Zoey."

"I know," I lie.

Sure, he may heal from his wounds, but he is still injured.

And he'll always have a scar from where a bullet hit him that was meant for me.

An hour later, and the entire surgical waiting room is empty besides my family and Lizzy. It is late, and my eyes feel heavier than they ever have before. As soon as one person yawns, it spreads like wildfire.

"I'm grabbing a coffee. Who wants one?" Tate asks as she stands and stretches.

"Me," Lulu says to our cousin. "Lots of sugar."

"No other way to have it," Tate replies. "Anyone else?"

Her question is met with silence. The last thing my heart needs right now is a dose of caffeine.

But before Tate can move, the doors open and a doctor walks in, removing his surgical cap.

My heart leaps in my chest, beating wildly. I study his face, trying to figure out if the news he is about to drop on us will be good or bad.

"Hunter Evan's family?" he asks.

"Yes," Lizzy replies.

We're the only people left, and deductive reasoning would make his guess that we are with Hunter accurate.

"He's out of surgery and in recovery. We'll be moving him to a room soon. Everything went well. As well as can be expected from a gunshot wound." The surgeon rubs a hand down his cheek. "The bullet missed all vital organs and was lodged in his gut. We were able to stop the bleeding, and his vital signs look good. The man is very lucky, though, a few inches either way and we'd be having a very different conversation."

"Oh, thank goodness," Lizzy breathes, practically deflating at the news.

I'm with her since I feel as if I can finally take my first full breath in hours. I had imagined the worst, preparing myself for the news that he didn't make it or would have some lasting injury.

"Thank you, Doctor," Lizzy adds. "When can we see him?"

"He'll most likely be out all night."

"Can I sit with him?" Lizzy asks.

"I'll have a nurse show you to his room, and you can stay with him."

Lizzy's eyes find me. "You're staying with me, right?"

I nod. "Wouldn't be anywhere else."

"We'll wait here," she tells him. "Thank you for everything, Doctor. Thank you for saving my brother's life."

"I'll be by tomorrow to check on him, but if all goes well, he should be out of here in a few days."

I blink, shocked at how quickly he'll be able to leave. "Really?"

"Once he's eating, drinking, and able to walk, he'll be able to go. It's always best to recover at home. Less chance of infection or other complications."

"Wow," Lizzy whispers and covers her mouth for a second. "That's great news."

"If you need anything, don't hesitate to ask," he tells us before he leaves.

"Maybe we should go," Mom says to Dad, touching his arm. "The girls have each other, and it's late. Are you okay with that, honey?"

The last question is to me. "Yeah, Mom. I'm going to stay with Lizzy. We'll be fine."

"I can stay," Mason offers, but he looks more tired than I feel.

"You go," Lizzy tells him. "Get some sleep and bring me a good cup of coffee tomorrow."

"I'll be here first thing," he tells her.

First thing to my cousin is after one in the afternoon. We're night owls. We always have been, but that's because of the bar life. Our days are typically getting started when everyone else's ends.

"Let me know if you need anything else," he says to her.

"Make that two cups," I tell him.

I doubt Lizzy or I will get any sleep tonight, and by the time the sun comes up, we'll need more than a little caffeine to function in any capacity.

"Call us if you need anything," Dad says to me as he climbs to his feet. "I can be here quick."

"Thanks, Daddy," I say, wrapping my arms around him as soon as I stand.

I can't imagine going through something like this without him around. Lizzy and Hunter don't have any parents. She has no one to lean on except for us in this moment.

"Try to get a little rest," Mom says as she gives me a

hug. "Don't push yourself too hard. Can't have you getting sick."

"I know, Mom. I won't overdo it."

She stares at me like she knows I'm lying, but she doesn't give me shit about it.

After all the hugs and kisses, along with a goodbye that takes forever, Lizzy and I are left alone. It's a quiet walk to Hunter's room as we wait for him to wake up.

CHAPTER 19
HUNTER

I OPEN my eyes and blink a few times.

Where the hell am I?

What happened?

I turn my head to the side, finding Lizzy and Zoey asleep in chairs next to my bed.

It takes my mind a moment to realize I'm not at home and that I'm in the hospital. The last thing I remember is kissing Zoey outside the Hook & Hustle—and then nothing.

I lift my arm, taking in the tubes and cords that are tangled together.

Am I sick?

Did I have a heart attack?

Something bigger than passing out or else I wouldn't be hooked up to a bunch of machines and…

I wince as I try to move. The muscles in my stomach protest at the slightest turn.

Shit.

My tongue is nearly stuck to the roof of my mouth

as I open my mouth to say something, but I stop when my lips stick together.

How long have I been like this?

Zoey opens her eyes and glances at me. She bolts upright as her gaze widens. "Lizzy, he's awake," she says, flying out of the chair to my side. "Hunter, oh my God, Hunter. You're awake."

She stares at me like it's a miracle that I opened my eyes. I wasn't nervous before, but suddenly, I'm aware that shit has gone way south and whatever happened to me isn't good.

"Am I..." I struggle to talk. My voice is more gravelly than it usually is, and it feels like I swallowed a mouthful of sand.

Lizzy's at Zoey's side before I can finish the sentence. "Thank God," Lizzy breathes as her shoulders fall forward like she's been holding the weight of the world on them.

"What..." I clear my throat, trying to force out whatever is lodged in there.

"Water," Zoey says as she reaches for something on the table next to me. "Here." She looks at me with so much emotion in her eyes, I wonder how close I really was to dying.

I take the cup from her hands, thankful my hands still work, but the cords make it hard to move as smoothly as usual. I lift my head, my abdominal muscles protesting as I do my best to move my mouth toward the cup. "Fuck," I groan, but it comes out as a whisper.

I can't take my eyes off my sister and Zoey as I take

a few small sips, even though I want to down the entire glass. They're staring at me, and it's completely unnerving. I feel like a goldfish stuck in a tank with an audience gawking at it as it swims around.

"What happened?" I ask as I place my head back on the pillow, and Zoey takes the cup out of my hands.

"Well…" Lizzy winces. "You're okay. I need you to know that." She tilts her head, giving me a weird smile.

Oh boy.

"You were shot," Zoey blurts out. "They got the bullet out, and you're going to be okay."

That's the second time they've used the word okay.

"Where?" I ask, but I already know. I've worked out a lot in my life, but my gut has never been as sore as it is right now.

"Your abdomen, but it didn't hit any vital organs," Lizzy says.

I beg to differ, based on how I feel. The bullet banged off everything.

It all comes back to me then.

"Fuck," I hiss as the memories flood back to me.

The bar.

Zoey.

Her twirling around in the snow.

The kiss.

God, the kiss.

The most amazing kiss of my entire life.

A loud noise.

Falling to the ground.

Zoey screaming over me.

The cold of the wet cement.

Everything goes black after that.

"Yeah," Lizzy says with a small laugh as she touches my hand. "I wasn't sure you were going to make it."

"You're here," I ask, my voice filled with disbelief. "How long was I out?" If she's here, it's been well over six hours because that's how long it takes to drive here under normal conditions.

"Twelve hours," Lizzy says. "I was here quick, though. I got on the last flight of the night."

"I'm sorry," I tell her, but it's not like I meant to be shot. What else is there to say when someone you love rushes to be by your bedside.

We went through enough trauma with our parents' deaths to last us a lifetime. The last thing she needed was to get a phone call that I'd been shot. If she isn't still in therapy, she's about to start going again.

"Don't be silly. It's not like you did this on purpose. Or did you mean to jump in front of a bullet?" she asks as she sits down on my bed near my legs.

"It wasn't on my bingo card for this year."

My sister smiles at me and rubs my legs. "Didn't think so."

"I let everyone know he's awake," Zoey says beside me, typing away on her phone.

"Who's everyone?"

"The family."

She didn't say her family, even though that's what she means.

"They were all here until you got out of surgery."

I must look at her funny because she adds, "My

parents, Tate, Mason, Lulu. They were all here waiting with your sister and me."

"Did everyone think I was going to die?" I ask her, hating that they all worried about me. But it's kind of nice too.

That's the rub when you lose your parents. Who's left to care about you? Sure, I have Lizzy, but that's a different kind of love and worry than a parent has for their child.

"We weren't sure until the surgery was over and the doctor talked to us. That was the first time I felt like I could breathe," Zoey explains.

I reach for her hand and take it in mine. "I hate that you were so worried."

"It's my fault," she says quickly and quietly, unable to meet my gaze.

"It's not your fault."

"It is, though." She sighs, trying to pull her hand out of mine.

"How is that?"

"It was Mark. He's the one who shot you."

I blink, staring at her. "Mark?" I ask, dumbfounded.

Zoey nods and squeezes her eyes shut.

"Flowers Mark? Creepy stalker Mark?"

"Yes," she whispers. "See? It's my fault."

My chest tightens at her words. It's not her fault. She can't control what that asshole does any more than I can, but I have a feeling that no matter what I say, she won't stop blaming herself.

"He's been arrested. The police were here early this morning to talk to Zoey about what happened, but they were able to confirm his ID from the security footage outside the bar," my sister explains.

It dawns on me then.

I probably wasn't his intended victim.

Zoey was.

Getting shot sucks, but never in a million years would I wish this on anyone else, especially Zoey. I'm glad, no matter how fucked up that sounds, that the bullet hit me and not her.

"Baby, look at me." I squeeze Zoey's hand, needing her to look into my eyes when I say these words.

For a moment, she doesn't look, but I squeeze her hand again.

When her gaze finally slides to mine, I say, "It's not your fault. And I'd take that bullet again if it meant that you were safe."

Zoey sucks in a breath as her eyes water, and a single tear slips down her cheek.

"He's in jail. He can't hurt you now," I tell her.

"But he hurt you," she replies.

If I could take her emotional hurt away, I'd do that too, but all I can do is use my words and hope that's enough.

"I'll heal. I'm alive, aren't I?"

"I thought you were going to die," she whispers as she uses her free hand to wipe her face.

"But I didn't. Mark's not an issue anymore, and I'm fine."

There's a knock on the open door of my hospital room before Mason stalks in carrying three cups of coffee in one of those annoying coffee carriers.

"Shit," he says as his eyes land on me. "I only brought three. Good to see you awake, brother."

I like the guy. Sure, he has asshole qualities, but so do I, and I'm almost positive that mine outnumber his.

"I'll stick with water for right now," I tell him as I watch my sister push off the bed and rush in his direction.

"You're the best," Lizzy says to him as she takes one cup from his hands. "I don't know how I'd function without this today."

"I got you a quad," Mason says, staring down at my sister in the way I know I stare at Zoey. "How long has he been awake?"

They're talking softly like I couldn't hear them, but the room is small and my hearing is good.

"Just a few minutes."

"Is he okay?" he asks her.

"He's good," she tells him.

"I can hear you," I grumble.

Zoey chuckles as she sits down next to me, careful not to jostle me too much.

"When can I go home?" I ask her, leaving Lizzy and Mason to talk.

"The doctor said, depending on how today goes, you may be able to get out of here tomorrow."

I groan. I was hoping she'd say today. Hospitals give me the creeps, and I'd rather crawl into my bed or hers than stay here.

"How today goes?"

"They need to make sure you can go to the bathroom and get around on your own. They want to make sure your lungs are working right too."

"Everything is fine," I tell her with a small smile. It's not, of course, but like hell would I say otherwise to her.

My gaze slides to my sister and Mason as they stand near the door.

"He was a huge help," Zoey says. "He picked up your sister from the airport so she wouldn't have to worry about getting to the hospital."

"That was nice of him," I tell her. Although he is a nice guy, it's also because he's sweet on my sister, and she's sweet on him too.

"Do you mind more visitors?" Zoey runs her fingernails down the underside of my arm, causing my eyes to close.

The feeling is too damn good. Everything about this experience is uncomfortable, and the small touches, the raking of the fingernails, hit the right spots.

"Who?" I ask softly.

"The family wants to come and see you."

My eyes fly open as my heart pounds in my chest. "No one told Amira, did they?"

Zoey shakes her head. "We didn't want to worry her."

I blow out a breath, hoping my heart will slow. "Good. Good. She doesn't need to know about this."

"I think she will the first time she sees you wince from pain," Zoey replies.

"I can hide it."

Zoey raises an eyebrow in challenge but doesn't say anything else about it.

"Visitors are fine."

It's nice, even. Lucio and Delilah are great people, and they have even better kids. Lulu and Zoey would make any parents proud. They're kind and caring with just enough saltiness not to be taken advantage of at every turn.

"Good, because they'll be here in five minutes. They're already inside the hospital." Zoey turns her head, glaring at Mason. "Hey. I hate to interrupt whatever is happening over there, but I'd like my coffee too."

Lizzy's hand touches Mason's arm, and he gives her a smile before his gaze moves to his cousin. "Coming right up." He stalks across the room in a few short steps, standing on the opposite side of my bed, and holds out a cup to his cousin. "Your order."

She snatches the cup from his hands and says, "Thank you." A second later, the cup is at her lips, and her eyes close like she's savoring every drop.

"You two should go home and get some real sleep," I tell Lizzy and Zoey. "I'll be fine here by myself."

"Oh no," Lizzy tells me. "We're not leaving until they kick us out."

"Which will be around eight tonight when visiting hours end. They made an exception for last night because you were knocked out," Zoey adds.

It's not that I want to be alone, but I know how uncomfortable it is to sleep in a hospital chair. They're running on adrenaline right now, but soon, it'll wane, and they'll be more like the walking dead.

There's a light tapping on the door before Zoey's

parents, Lulu, Oliver, Harlow, Tate, and Zoey's grandparents walk into the room.

I'm taken aback by the number of people who can cram into a small space. And they did it to see me. Even when my parents were alive, we were a small unit. We didn't have much family besides the four of us to speak of, and if we landed in the hospital, visitors were few and far between.

"You look good, son," Lucio says as he walks to stand next to Mason with his wife on his arm.

Delilah is beautiful. Lulu and Zoey look so much like her, there's no doubting who their mother is.

"Oh, sweetie. You're looking good," Delilah says as she holds on to Lucio's arm.

"Let me see that man," a voice I could clock from across the room without even looking says as Zoey's grandmother scoots around everyone to come to the side of the bed where Zoey's sitting. "As handsome as ever." She smiles at me.

I can't help but look at her and wonder what it would've been like to have had grandparents of my own. Just like my parents, their parents died young, but not in the same tragic way. I hadn't thought much about growing up without them, but after being around the Gallo family, I know I missed out on so much when it comes to family members.

"It's good to see you, beautiful," I tell her, giving her a soft smile.

She waves her hand at me. "His mind's working good too."

Zoey chuckles as she leans over and gives her

grandma a kiss on the cheek. "Thanks for coming, Gram."

"No place else we'd rather be," she says, cradling Zoey's cheek in her hand.

"Getting shot sucks," Zoey's grandfather says.

My eyes widen as I stare at him. When I look at an older person, it's easy to forget they were young once and had lives we can never fully grasp.

When I look at him, I don't see a man who could've been shot. He looks like he's always sat in a recliner, sipping a nice glass of wine, doing a crossword puzzle.

"You got shot in the leg," Betty tells her husband. "It's hardly the same."

"The woman has no empathy," he says to no one in particular. "And don't forget about my ass too."

Wait. He wasn't just shot once, but two times? How in the world?

"That one wasn't that bad," she replies.

He gives her a hard stare. "It wasn't your ass."

She waves her hand wildly in the air, dismissing him. "Men," she mumbles. "Some are big babies."

"Grandpa, why were you shot twice?" Zoey asks him.

I'm happy the focus is on him and off me. It helps to keep the pressure away from me.

"A bad business deal," he says.

"Bar business?" I ask, confused.

Betty clucks her tongue. "Sal has an illustrious past."

"Illustrious and criminal," Lucio adds.

Sal shrugs. "Times were different."

"You on the up-and-up now?" Mason asks with his

head tilted, like he knows something everyone else doesn't.

"For the most part," Sal answers. "Most of the time."

I start to laugh, but when a pain shoots through my middle, it quickly dies.

Sal's gaze drops to me. "I'll take an ass and a leg over the stomach any day of the week."

"That ain't no lie," I tell him as I try to adjust in the bed to find a better position.

"When you go home, we'll make sure your fridge is stocked so you don't have to worry about cooking," Delilah says to me, placing her hand on my arm. "We want you to focus on healing."

"You're too kind, Mrs. Gallo," I say.

"Delilah," she corrects me.

"I'll be able to cook."

"Nonsense," she says, shaking her head. "You take as long as you need to get well. Don't push yourself."

"You get one week off, and then it's back to the grind," Tate, my boss and Zoey's cousin, interrupts. "If you need more than that, we're going to have a problem."

I know she's teasing. Tate is a great person, and I am lucky to have landed a spot in her shop and to have her as a boss.

"I'll be back in a week. I can't sit around much longer than that," I tell her.

I've never been one to be idle. If I have to stay home and nurse myself back to health for a solid week, I'm liable to go insane.

"I shuffled your clients around to later appointments, but you know I'm kidding about the week, right? Take as long as you need, Hunter. If people are in a hurry, I'll handle the extra load, or Timber will. We got you, buddy."

Who knew that when I met Tate, she'd become such a big part of my life, and that down the line, I'd fall hard for her cousin? Maybe someday we'll become family in the truest sense of the word.

I sober at my thoughts. Did I just go there? Zoey and I have only kissed, and I let my mind drift to something more and a future.

Maybe the anesthesia is messing with my head, because yesterday I kissed Zoey for the first time, and I wasn't thinking about a future together.

Life is short. I know that, but I've still ignored it because I am young enough that I sometimes allow myself that luxury, even though it's stupid. Age doesn't matter when it comes to death. It comes for each of us in its own way or time.

CHAPTER 20
ZOEY

THE LAST FIVE days of my life have been the craziest ever. And that's saying a lot, after the first bit of chaos Mark caused in my life and my family's.

Hunter has been home for four days, and he's healing well. He's been up and about, refusing to stay on the couch or in bed most of the day. The man has ants in his pants, and relaxation isn't part of his personality.

You wouldn't have to twist my arm to make me stay in bed. I could binge the hell out of television series and books.

"Are you sure you two are going to be okay?" Lizzy asks as she zips up her coat.

"I think we'll manage," Hunter tells her, rubbing my feet as we both lie on the couch, but on opposite ends.

This feels a little bit like being a kid again and his mom is heading out for the evening but she's also reluctant to leave us alone.

"You go have fun, but not too much," Hunter says,

turning the tables on her. "And be home at a reasonable hour."

Lizzy ignores him like all sisters do when their brothers are being ridiculous. "Don't wait up." She's gone a moment later.

"You think she'll come home tonight?" Hunter asks me as he presses the pad of his thumb into the soft part of my foot.

I nearly melt into the couch as I let out a little moan. "Maybe," I whisper.

"Don't make noises like that," he tells me, his voice rough and gravelly.

"I can't help it. That feels too good."

"Damn it. I wish I didn't have these stitches to worry about."

I raise an eyebrow as I stare down the length of the couch at him. "Because you'd what?"

"Finish where we left off."

"We could still kiss," I offer, remembering the way my toes curled when he did it the first and only time.

"Come here," he says and releases my foot.

I do my best not to groan in protest because the foot massage was too good. I'm a sucker for a foot rub, and getting one without having to go to a spa is nearly impossible since I swore off relationships.

I crawl over his legs, careful not to touch his middle. He is still healing, and he doesn't have a follow-up with the surgeon until next week. Light physical activity is allowed, but getting hot and heavy didn't seem to be included on that list.

And I want Hunter. I mean, I *want* him. There is a

hunger inside me to taste his lips again that I don't think I've ever felt for another human being in my entire life.

My hands are on the couch as I hold my body up, careful not to touch him.

"I'm not breakable," he whispers as my face gets closer to his.

He may not be breakable, but I'm liable to do some damage if I touch the wrong spot or put too much weight on him.

"I don't want to hurt you."

He wraps his fingers around my head as he slides his palm against my neck. Goose bumps break out across my skin as I gaze into his deep blue eyes.

I see a hunger burning in them that I'm sure matches mine.

"Baby, you can't hurt me. Stop talking and kiss me."

"Kiss me," I tell him, repeating the words I said before this nightmare began.

He pulls me down, and my lips crash into his, sending a shiver down my spine as his fingertips curl into my scalp.

His lips are soft, and they have a sweetness to them. He tastes like vanilla from the cupcakes I got from Tilly's shop, which she insisted I bring to Hunter to help in his recovery.

He jolts underneath me, and I freeze. I open my eyes, seeing his wince, but our mouths are still connected.

He's not going to stop. He wants this as much as I

do, but one of us must be the responsible adult and not let our libido control the situation.

I pull back and Hunter groans. "Wait," he says, not releasing his grip on me. "Don't stop."

"We can't do this." I study his face as I say those words, telling myself to hold steady and firm.

"We can. I'm fine."

"I hurt you." My arms shake as I try to hold myself up high enough that there's no risk I can hurt him again.

"You didn't hurt me, Zoey. My muscle pulled a stitch. It happens."

"It wouldn't have happened if we weren't…"

"Kissing?"

"Well, yeah," I whisper, unable to take my eyes off his face.

"Kissing never killed anyone."

"I'm sure it has killed someone."

He lets out a heavy sigh. "Is there anything I can say to make you kiss me again?"

"No."

He releases his grip on me, and I push myself back to the safety of my side of the couch. "What's that face? Are you pouting?"

His frown deepens. "What if I am?"

"Men are so dramatic."

"I was shot. I'm injured. I'm allowed to be a bit dramatic."

I roll my eyes and laugh. "Now you admit you're still in pain?"

"I didn't say I was in pain."

"What do you want to do?"

"Make out," he answers with a wry grin.

"Not happening. Pick something else."

Hunter scratches at his beard, which has become a little unruly in the last few days.

"I could trim your beard," I offer.

"Will you sit on my lap while you do it?"

I chuckle, knowing he's going to get handsy, but I like the idea anyway. "Will you keep your hands to yourself?"

He smirks and lifts his hands. "I can't promise that."

"I'll get everything ready," I tell him before I get off the couch, pulling my sweater tighter to keep out the chill.

I'm over winter, and it's barely even started. This is the best part of the season. When the Christmas trees are up and the holiday lights cover the city in an entirely different color glow. There's an excitement to the city, but once the new year starts, January comes in like a bear and time seems to stand still.

"Everything is under my sink."

"Got it," I call out as I head toward his bathroom.

The layout of his place is the same as mine, which makes it easy to navigate. His bathroom is surprisingly tidy and clean, unlike many of the guys I know. But it's also bland and sterile. Obviously, Lizzy didn't decorate it. Everything is white, including the hand towel hanging on the wall next to the sink.

I kneel and open the cabinet under the sink. Everything inside is organized in a particular way. Tallest items in the back and the shortest toward the front. This is something I can only see Lizzy doing.

I grab the electric razor and a pair of scissors and a comb from a cup nearby. Men live entirely different lives. Most of the items in the cabinet are cleaning products. It's so unlike mine, which is bursting at the seams with makeup, skin care, brushes of every kind, and more.

"Find what you need?" Hunter asks from the living room.

I quickly close the cabinet door, not wanting him to think that I'm snooping through his things. I don't bother yelling back because it's only a few short steps until I'm where he can see me from his spot on the couch.

"I think I got everything. Want help up?"

He shakes his head as he starts to move at a glacial pace. He doesn't wince as he turns his body, but I know he wants to. The level of concentration on his face tells me every movement is measured to reduce the amount of pain.

I've never been shot or had surgery, but I've fallen on my ass too many times to count. I know when your body's sore, any little thing can send a slice of pain through you that can take your breath away.

Instead of staring at him, I grab a chair from the dining area and place it near the couch, so he doesn't need to move very far.

"Shit, I forgot a towel," I say before running back to the bathroom to grab one.

When I open the linen closet, I'm surprised the big

towels aren't white like everything else in the bathroom. They're black, which is a stark contrast to everything else. Still not a color, but close enough.

By the time I get back to the living room, he's sitting in the chair, taking measured breaths.

"Your grandpa was right. Getting shot sucks. But a shot to the ass or the leg would've been easier. You don't realize how much you use your stomach for. This is like the worst abdominal workout ever."

"Poor guy," I say as I wrap a towel around the front of him to catch the little hairs, so he isn't itchy later. I'd seen my dad do this when he needed a last-minute trim before running out the door.

"Sit," he tells me, patting his legs with a smile.

The man is handsome. And on top of that, he took a bullet for me from a madman. He hasn't complained once either.

I settle most of my weight on him as I sit on his thighs, but I keep the tips of my toes pinned to the floor so I don't give him every pound. I'm not a skinny girl, and the last thing I want to do is put more pressure on him than necessary.

His hands settle on the top of my hips near my waist. He pulls me forward, leaving very little room for me to work.

"Hunter," I chastise and shake my head.

He chuckles. "You were too far away."

"Now, I'm too close." I scoot back a few inches and stare down at his face.

His eyes almost take my breath away. They're dark

blue in the dimness of the apartment. They look like a turbulent sea right before a thunderstorm.

He stares into my eyes as I comb out his beard, making sure every errant hair is easy to spot. Every so often, I let my gaze dip to his, and the way he's looking at me almost takes the air right out of my lungs.

"You're beautiful," he whispers as his thumbs stroke a small patch of exposed skin between my T-shirt and jeans.

"You're making it hard to concentrate."

"That's the point." He smirks, moving all the hairs around his mouth.

"You need to hold still. I'd hate it if you needed more stitches."

"Don't cut me."

"Don't move," I tell him as I open and close the scissors a few times, making sure he sees them to drive the point home.

I have no idea what I'm doing. I've never trimmed anyone's beard, but it can't be that hard. I've cut my own bangs hundreds of times, but it isn't always successful, and I've spent weeks with hair that was way too short.

"It's impossible in this position," he says.

"I need five minutes." I lean forward, snipping a few hairs hanging too low around his jawline.

"You've got five, and then I get five."

I glance up, meeting his gaze. "You get five for what?"

"Kissing you."

I go back to the task at hand, trying to ignore the need in my body. "We tried that. It didn't work."

"Oh, it worked, but this is a better position."

"You're not in any pain?"

"None."

"No more talking," I tell him. "I need to focus."

"Lips are sealed…for now."

He's impossible. Men are impossible. They have one thing on their minds. It doesn't matter if they've had a hole blown in them, they'll still want sex, no matter how painful the experience may be for them.

I spend the next five minutes working on his beard without looking him in the eyes. I don't dare focus on anything except the task at hand.

Hunter's hands don't leave me the entire time. They're slowly caressing my body through my jeans, and I want to melt into him, but I force myself to stay upright and focused.

When I'm finally finished, I set the scissors down and lean back, taking in my work. "I think it looks great."

"Am I pretty now?" he teases, his mouth twitching at the corners.

"You were always pretty."

"There's nothing in the world prettier than you, Zoey."

My heart flutters. The man is laying it on thick. And it's working. No matter how hard I try to tell myself he needs more time to heal and that I shouldn't plant my lips on his, I lose the battle because my body says otherwise.

He tears the towel off his chest and drops it to the floor. "Where did we leave off?" he asks, gliding his hands up my back underneath my shirt. His palms are hot, blazing a path across my skin and causing my body to ignite.

"We shouldn't."

"We should."

"Hunter."

"I earned the kiss. Bullet and all."

He's playing dirty. He can dangle that bit of history in front of me forever, and it'll work too.

"One kiss."

"A long one," he adds with a slight nod as he pulls my body closer.

Our middles meet, and I can feel the hard length of him pressing against my center. The bullet may have damaged his stomach muscles, but this one is perfectly fine. Better than that. He's big, thick, and long. Not obscenely large like he could make adult films for a living with a bunch of women thirsting after an impossible-to-fit size.

I lean forward, wrapping my arms around his shoulders, careful not to push against his stomach. I'm gentle as I press my lips to his, the familiar taste of the cupcakes from earlier meeting my mouth.

He curls his fingers into my back, pulling me flush against him. But this time, he doesn't flinch or freeze, only deepens the kiss. His lips demand more than I was planning to give him, but I can't deny him anything.

I open farther, driving my tongue deeper, sliding it against his, and I moan.

Only a few more days until he gets the okay from the doctors. I can hold out that long... Can't I?

CHAPTER 21
HUNTER

ZOEY WANTED to cancel her holiday party, but I wouldn't let her. She said my shooting put a damper on the holiday, but I look at it another way. I survived, and that is a hell of a thing to celebrate this Christmas.

I couldn't help with setting up, but I could plant my ass in a chair and talk to people while the rest of them drink themselves into a holiday stupor.

"How are you feeling, baby?" Delilah, Zoey's mom, asks as she places her hand on my cheek. It's something my own mother did when she was concerned about me.

"I'm good," I tell her, studying her features and the similarities between her and her daughters, especially Zoey. "Better than good."

"Has Zoey been taking good care of you?"

My face heats as I remember the make-out session last night. "She's been doing a hell of a job."

"Good. Good." She pulls her hand back as her husband slides his arm around her middle and draws her close.

"Hunter," Mr. Gallo says with a curt nod. The man is nice, but he's a guy, and I'm the enemy because I'm dating his daughter, even if I took a bullet for her.

When Amira starts dating, I won't be friendly with her suitors either. At least, not at first. It's a tough line to walk as a father. You don't want to be a complete asshole, but you also want the guy to know that you know what's running through his mind too.

The very thought of Amira as a grown-ass woman being pursued by most of the slimeballs out there makes me irrationally angry.

"Stitches good?" he asks me.

I nod. "I go to the surgeon in a few days, but they feel good."

"You're young. You'll heal quick," he replies.

"I'm almost back to my old self."

And I mean that literally. I wish I healed at the same speed I did in my twenties, but now that I have a few toes into my thirties, everything has slowed down, my body's ability to heal itself in a timely manner included.

"I brought you some Italian Wedding Soup. It's in Zoey's fridge for you to eat tomorrow," Delilah says, ignoring our conversation.

"It's one of my favorites," Mr. Gallo adds.

"I saved some for you, sweetie."

He beams at his wife. I can see the love in his eyes. I want that. The long-lasting love that only deepens over time. Zoey has great role models in her parents. Sure, mine loved each other, but looking back on things, they were more comfortable than in true, deep love.

Lizzy strolls over carrying a plate nearly overflowing with food. "Grandma Betty says you need to eat every last morsel."

I like the sound of that coming from my sister. Grandma Betty.

The warmth of the Gallos is unmatched.

I take the plate from my sister's hands and nearly choke. "Who can eat all this?"

Mr. Gallo touches my shoulder and laughs. "You'll find a way, and you have a few hours. I'm sure you can fit it in there somewhere."

"This is a lot," I tell them.

"She said you need the calories to heal," Lizzy explains. "I'm just the delivery person. Take it up with her if you have a problem."

"Ma thinks food fixes all problems," Mr. Gallo tells me. "You'll get used to it."

I hope I'm around long enough for that to be true. I've never felt as welcomed into a group of practical strangers as I have with them. I could see myself sliding into this life without an issue and never looking back.

It doesn't hurt that Zoey's an amazing woman who has my full attention. We've both been through enough shit to last a lifetime, and we could use a little peace and quiet, along with a huge dose of happiness.

"Speaking of food, I'm starving," Mr. Gallo says before ushering his wife away.

"Their parents are cool," Lizzy says as she takes the seat next to me. "I can see why Lulu and Zoey are good people."

"Who's not good people in this family?" I ask her, picking up a square piece of pizza that's hanging off the side of my plate. It doesn't have sauce, but it's got some caramelized onions, sprinkled cheese, and not much else from the looks of it.

"The grandpa is debatable."

I nearly choke on my first bite when she says that. I chew quickly, trying to enjoy the flavors, which are way more complex than I expected. The pizza is well seasoned with salt, pepper, and something else I can't place.

"Stop, Liz. He's good too."

"Two bullets would say otherwise. And not at the same time either." She purses her lips as she stares at him across the room. "It's so wild."

"We're all young once."

She lifts a glass of champagne to her lips, still watching him. "You think he's out of the life?"

"Who knows," I say before tearing off another chunk of the pizza with my teeth. "Not my problem or my business."

"I've watched way too much TV."

"You have. You had a period when you couldn't get enough of those damn mafia shows."

"They're top tier, but now I'm wondering how true they were."

"Ask him."

Her eyes widen as she turns her head to look at me. "I can't just ask him about his criminal past."

"Why not? He seems open about it."

She holds up her half-empty glass. "If I have a few more of these, I just may."

Mason spots us from across the room, grabs a bottle

off the counter, and makes a beeline toward us. My sister got home late last night, well after two in the morning, but I knew she was physically safe with him. By the way she was beaming this morning, I imagine the night went well, but in no way do I want any details.

"Refill?" Mason asks, holding out the champagne bottle toward my sister's glass.

"Yes, please." She smiles up at him like the man is a walking dream.

He glances at me. "Want one?"

I shake my head. "Can't."

"Right," he says with a dip of his head. "Bullet."

"Bullet," I repeat and find the fork Lizzy set next to me after she gave me the plate of food.

"You going to eat all that?" he asks me with a look of concern.

"Grandma Betty said he has to."

Mason laughs as he moves to stand beside my sister, placing the champagne bottle on the bookshelf behind our seats.

I stare out across Zoey's place, taking in all the work she did this week, preparing for the party. On top of helping me, she pulled it off. She said her family helped this year because she needed backup. I feel slightly guilty that I took up her time and couldn't help myself.

Christmas lights are everywhere, and the tree that I helped Mason carry in is filled with ornaments, looking like something straight out of a catalogue. The woman outdid herself with very little free time.

"You want to go out again later?" Mason asks Lizzy.

I don't turn my head, and I pretend I didn't hear him ask her. She's grown, and it's none of my business as long as he doesn't break her heart or use her and then throw her out like a piece of trash.

"Yeah. Same place as last night?" she asks.

"You got it," he says.

I have no idea where they went. I didn't ask, and she wasn't forthcoming with information. If and when she wants to share, I'll listen, but until then, I hear nothing and I see nothing either. Every adult is entitled to privacy, but if I had to bet, there's a Gallo in this room who already knows all the details.

"We can ditch the party early," Mason tells her as he kneels in front of my sister since there isn't an extra chair.

I busy myself with my food, focusing on Zoey as she works the room, making sure everyone has food and drinks.

Soft Christmas music is playing throughout the entire place, but not loud enough to drown out the conversation. Everyone's talking in small groups with lots of touches and laughs.

Zoey's surrounded herself by a large group of people, both friends and family, who seem to thoroughly love being around one another. I don't know if I've ever experienced something like this before, but I love every single bit of it.

My mom could host a great party, but nothing quite as big as this. She did the same as Zoey, throwing something lavish for her closest friends around the holidays. But instead of fifty people, there would be ten. I have fond memories of that period from my childhood, when I would crack open my door and watch the adults as they celebrated.

My eyes catch on Tate across the room, and I give her a quick chin lift as she talks to Timber. She touches his arm, saying something to him before they turn as one to look at me. A moment later, they're moving through the crowd, heading toward me.

"Yo," Timber says with a chin dip.

"Merry Christmas, Hunter," Tate says and bends down to kiss my cheek.

"Shop's been boring without you," Timber says, pursing his lips. "It's all girl things all the time. I need your testosterone back, bud."

"I'll be there this week."

As she straightens, Tate turns her head with what I can only assume is a glare. "It's not girl things all the time. What the hell does that even mean?"

Timber shrugs and takes a pull from his beer.

"He's right about one thing. We need you back there, but I don't want to rush your recovery," she says and takes the extra beer Timber had been holding in his other hand. "Thank you." She tips the beer toward him before she puts it against her lips and drains half the bottle.

Timber grumbles but doesn't argue. If I didn't know better, I'd think Tate and Timber were brother and sister. They bicker like siblings most of the time at work and even out of it too.

"Baby, you're going hard," Wylder says, coming up

behind Tate. He wraps his arm around her middle and hauls her against him. "You may want to slow down."

"It's so hot in here," she says and takes a hand to jerk the neck of her sweater back and forth to get more airflow. "Why am I so hot while you all look comfortable?"

"Um," Wylder mumbles as he flattens a hand on Tate's stomach. "I remember the last time you were always hot."

The bottle is against her lips, and she freezes. "Oh God," she breathes against the glass as her eyes widen. "No."

The look on Tate's face would be laughable if it weren't filled with absolute and complete panic.

"I can't be," she whispers, moving the beer away from her lips. "I can't."

"Baby, would it be the worst thing?" Wylder asks, smiling against the skin of her neck.

Tate whips around so fast, Wylder stumbles backward, but he catches himself before he trips over a table filled with appetizers.

"If you knocked me up…" she says, poking him in the chest so hard, he flinches.

"Darlin', I think you were an active participant in the process."

My mouth forms an O as I gawk at them. I know this isn't going to go well for him. Poor guy. I might not be the smartest man on earth, but I know that answer isn't going to win him any brownie points.

Tate rears back and sucker-punches Wylder in the shoulder. "If I'm pregnant again, I'm going to…"

He reaches out and grabs her arm, hauling her toward him. "Think of a little one close to Willow's age. Maddy and Hazel are so much older than her."

Tate's shoulders sag as she stares up at her husband. "That would be nice."

"And we planned on another. So what if we move up our timeline a little."

"I guess," she says, but there's very little enthusiasm in her voice.

"We'll grab a test on our way home, but maybe you're hot because you have on a sweater and a long-sleeved shirt. It doesn't help that there are dozens of people in here, generating all kinds of heat."

"I've been hot for a week now," she tells him and then sighs. "I'm pregnant. I know it. I don't even need a test. It'll be fine. I'll be fine. My tits are never going to recover, though."

I bite back my laughter because the last thing I need is Tate wanting to poke me right in my wound.

Wylder pulls her into a hug, nuzzling his face against her neck. "Your tits are great."

"They were," she mumbles into his shirt.

Zoey pops up out of nowhere. Wylder's large frame had hidden her until she moved around him, seeming to appear out of thin air.

"Hey," she says with the biggest smile.

My heart leaps at her nearness. No one's ever had that effect on me before. It's the oddest thing.

"Hey," I hold out a hand, balancing the half-eaten plate on my leg. "You need help with anything?"

I'm sick of sitting around and doing nothing. I've

never been one to be still for too long, and this healing bullshit got old days ago. I am almost ready to jump out of my own skin if I don't get my ass moving.

"There's nothing to do."

"I can clean up," I offer, grasping at straws at this point.

"That's later, and if you want to help, you can do light duty. I'll be up all night putting this place back together."

"I'll stay," I tell her without a moment's hesitation.

I'd do anything to spend more time with her and to move my body around. The more I move, the less sore I find myself the next day. The worst part of the day is when I wake up. My body's been still for far too long, and getting my stomach muscles to move again without hurting takes more than a few minutes.

"I can stay too," Lizzy offers.

Mason clears his throat and stares at my sister's profile. "Actually, we have plans. Remember, Lizzy?"

She nods slowly. "Oh, right. We'll both stay and help for a bit before we head out for the night."

Mason's lips flatten. "Sure. We can help for a little bit."

"Good boy," Lizzy whispers with a small smirk.

"As you wish, queen," he replies with a dip of his head.

I draw my eyebrows in as I stare at them. What in the world? When I turn back to Zoey, she's looking at them the exact same way.

"I don't know what that is, but alrighty," she says with a shake of her head. "Thanks." Those words are meant for them, but they aren't paying attention to us anymore.

Zoey pitches her thumb over her shoulder to where Tate and Wylder are still in deep conversation. "What's that about?"

"She thinks she's pregnant."

Zoey pales. "Oh shit."

"Yeah, that was basically Tate's response too."

"The first delivery wasn't easy for her. I don't think I could do two. Hell, I don't even want to do one."

"No?" I ask, surprised.

She shakes her head. "I watched Lulu give birth to Harlow. That experience is burned into my brain forever. I can't imagine."

"I won't lie to you and tell you it isn't that bad. I don't have the right body parts to make that statement."

"Thank you." Zoey places her hand on my shoulder and leans forward, coming eye-to-eye with me. "Maybe we can do more kissing while we clean up later." She waggles her eyebrows.

My hand finds her chin, tipping her head so our mouths are lined up. "How about one right now? A quick one before anyone notices."

She doesn't even think about it. Her mouth touches mine, soft and gentle, completely unlike last night. But she does it without hesitation in front of her entire family and all her friends.

"Thanks," I say with a husky voice as soon as her lips leave mine.

She gives me a sweet smile. "There's more of that to come later."

I can't freaking wait to get the okay from the doctor. It doesn't matter to me if Zoey wants to have sex or not. I want something more than kissing to be an option. I won't push her, though. Everything will be on her timeline, after what happened to her with Mark.

It's a miracle she's even given me the time of day. I know she pushed the boundaries of her comfort zone already by the small amount of kissing we've done. Anything else will be a bonus.

"Zoey," her grandmother calls out from the kitchen island, and somehow her voice can be heard above the music and chatter.

"Got to go. Later," Zoey says, giving my shoulder a squeeze before she stalks away, giving me the perfect view of her ass.

Later, indeed.

CHAPTER 22
ZOEY

LULU: *Today's the day.*

I stare down at my sister's message as I straighten my hair. I have to be out of the house in thirty minutes so I'm not late for my night shift at the bar.

Mason's been picking up my slack while I've been helping Hunter since he was released from the hospital.

I pick up my phone, typing out a quick message. I'm going to play stupid. I know what day it is.

Today, Hunter goes to the doctor. He should be there now, hopefully getting the "all clear" from the surgeon for his return to full physical activity.

Me: What?

It doesn't take more than a second for my sister to reply.

Lulu: For you to get some D, baby.

I roll my eyes and laugh. Leave it to my sister to be so eloquent with her words.

Lulu: No more Sister Zoey. Dusting off those cobwebs.

Hunter and I have been kissing like a couple of high

school kids for the last few days. It's been hard not to do anything more, and no one is more surprised about that than I.

I never thought I'd trust someone again, but Hunter's made that possible. He's safe. I feel that deep down in my bones.

I grab my flat iron, ignoring my sister's message. It wasn't that long ago she told me I needed to join a convent. It wasn't that I didn't want a boyfriend. It was that I didn't know who to trust.

I don't know how it happened, but it did. Hunter made it easy. Throw Amira into the mix, and there was no way I could resist the guy. Watching him dote on his little girl made me realize he wasn't a threat to me physically or to my heart.

Instead of my sister replying in our private chat, she moves the conversation over to the family chat.

Lulu: I heard someone's been kissing someone.

I shake my head. I love my family, but sometimes the need for everyone to know everything all the time is a bit overwhelming. There's no such thing as privacy.

Mason: Who told you about me and Lizzy?

I blink a few times, rereading his message. I knew they were flirting and had hung out, but Mason's been quiet about everything if he's been locking lips with Lizzy.

The shock must've worn off quickly for everyone else because the messages start rolling in at a fast and furious pace.

Lulu: OMG. What? When? You've been holding out.

Mason: Shit. I thought you were talking about me. Carry on.

Tate: Carry on? Um, no, sir. We want details.

Mason: A true gentleman never kisses and tells.

Lulu: Can you hear me snorting from there?

Mason: I've grown up.

My cousin is laughable at times, but he's trying. He claims he's ready to leave his single ways behind him and that he wants to settle down. I hope he's not leading Lizzy on. If he breaks her heart, I'll be so disappointed in him.

Nino: Who's Lizzy?

God, I love my cousin, Nino. He's the most aloof member of the family. He minds his own business, unlike the rest of us. It's probably because he's an only child, but he's also totally spoiled.

Lulu: Hunter's sister.

Nino: Who's Hunter?

Amelia: Nino, what the hell is wrong with you?

Nino: I don't pay attention to y'all.

Tate: Obviously.

Nino: I've got my own life. I don't need to be in yours too.

I love my cousin. He's one of my favorites. It's probably because he does mind his own business.

Lulu: Hunter is Zoey's boyfriend.

Lulu's message is the first time I've seen Hunter called that. I've never spoken the words out loud either, but he is my boyfriend, isn't he? I guess that's a conversation we need to have before we go any further because I don't want to get my heart broken either.

Nino: Cool.

Tate: So, who else is kissing?

Lulu: Hunter and Zoey.

Nino: Wow. She's kissing her boyfriend. Mind-blowing news, Lulu.

Lulu: Shut up, Nino. Jagoff.

Nino: Peace out.

Amelia: Zoey—did you two…

Mason: I don't want to hear this. Go to a girls' only chat and leave the rest of us alone.

I chuckle. I don't want to hear about his sex life either, but that doesn't mean I don't want to make him immensely uncomfortable.

Me: No. Not yet.

Mason: Ick. I'm gone. Bye.

Tate: I'm pregnant.

"Holy shit," I say, staring at my phone screen.

It's not a total surprise. Hunter told me what happened at the party, and I was certain she was, although I hoped for her sake she wasn't.

Amelia: Congrats, cousin! How exciting.

Tate: Yeah.

Brax: Don't sound overly excited there, Tater Tot.

Tate: You squeeze a human out of your body and tell me how excited you'd be.

Brax: Valid point.

Lulu: Other chat. Now!

I swipe my screen, moving to the girls' chat, which always has a very different conversation from the general family chat all my cousins and I have.

We talk about everything that would make the men

in the family lose their absolute shit. Periods. Cramps. Boyfriends. Husbands.

Lulu: Do you know when you're due?

Tate: No. I have an appointment this week to hopefully nail down a due date.

Me: Congrats, cousin.

Tate: I'm so mad at Wylder.

I laugh again and shake my head. Like it's entirely his fault. She didn't fall on his dick.

Lulu: You're ridiculous. I want another one. Maybe I can talk Oliver into it, and we can have babies around the same time.

Me: You're bananas.

Lulu: It's worth every ounce of pain.

Me: I don't believe you.

Tate: She's kind of right, Zoey, but I wouldn't do it without a kick-ass epidural. I don't know how people did it in the olden days.

This entire conversation reminds me to take my birth control pill. If Hunter and I are going to have sex soon, which I hope like hell we are, I didn't want to wind up like Tate.

Amelia: I hope it's a little girl.

Tate: A healthy baby is all I care about, but a boy would be nice. We already have three girls.

Lulu: Wylder is the best girl dad.

Tate: He is. There's something special about girl dads.

The conversation makes me think of Hunter. The very thought of him makes my blood pressure rise and my stomach flip with excitement.

Me: Got to go. Heading to the bar. Congrats again, Tate.

I close my texts as I leave my bathroom. I make it two steps before I back up, making sure I unplugged my straightener. I make a mental note that it's out of the wall, so I don't have a panic attack later.

I slip on my boots and grab my coat before running out the door toward the elevator. When the doors open, Hunter's the first thing I see.

He's staring at the floor, and when he tips his head up and his eyes meet mine, a smile spreads across his face. "All clear," he says as he stalks out of the elevator and grabs me in a hug.

I soak him in, inhaling the cologne I hadn't seen in his bathroom when I was in there. "That's great news." I wrap my arms around him, happy that his healing is going well, especially since I'm the reason he was injured in the first place.

"I'll come get you after work," he says into my hair.

"You don't have to do that."

He pulls back, staring at me. "You're not walking home alone."

"But I'm safe. Mark's in jail…soon to be prison."

"It doesn't matter. I'm not letting my girl walk home late at night by herself."

My stomach flips like a swarm of butterflies has taken flight. "Oh. Okay." It's all I can say.

I guess that answers that question. I am, in fact, Hunter's girlfriend.

"Lizzy's leaving tomorrow. I thought maybe tonight I'd stay at your place."

I bite the corner of my lip, knowing exactly what that means. "More than kissing?"

He smirks. "More than kissing."

"Fuck yes," I say and press my lips to his, giving him a taste of what's to come. "I got to go. I'm late."

"Go," he says, dropping his hands from me. "I'll be there later."

"I'll be waiting," I say and give his ass a swat before I step onto the elevator, leaving him smiling and shaking his head in the hallway outside our places.

———

My shift at the bar drags. Every minute feels like an hour. We're busy, which helps, but unlike most nights, it doesn't make the time pass any quicker.

"Sweetie, your man's here," Carly, a newer waitress we hired a few months ago, says to me as she points toward the entrance.

My heart leaps at the sight of him. It is such an odd feeling. Will it ever go away, or is this how my body will permanently react to him every time I see him for the rest of our lives?

I freeze. Did I just think about long-term? Not just long-term, but forever? Holy shit. I didn't think I'd let my mind go there this quickly, but that's the Hunter effect.

I stare at him as he stalks across the bar in what seems like a few short steps. If I didn't know better, I would've never guessed he was shot a week ago. The man is walking with a purpose, and the purpose is me.

"I'm not ready to go," I tell him as he slides onto the empty stool in front of me.

"I know. I came for a drink. I needed to get out of the apartment. I already stopped at the shop to talk to Tate."

"Oh. Beer?"

"A beer would be great." He taps his fingers on the wood, glancing around.

The regulars are staring at him. They were here when he got shot because they don't leave until we force them out every single night. This is their home away from home.

"Hey. Hey. What's up, superman? Up and about already?" Marvin asks, glancing down the bar in Hunter's direction.

"That's Marv," I tell Hunter as I grab a beer from the cooler underneath the bar.

"I'm up and about, Marv," Hunter replies.

"A bullet can't stop you," Marv adds.

Hunter leans forward when I place his beer down in front of him. "Am I imagining things, or are people staring at me?"

"You're not imagining anything," I tell him.

Marv climbs off his stool and walks toward Hunter.

"Oh boy," I whisper, wondering what's going to come out of Marv's mouth next. It could honestly be anything, especially since he's six beers deep.

Marv holds out one hand and touches Hunter's shoulder with his other. "I need to shake the hand of the man who saved our Zoey's life."

Hunter's face turns the deepest shade of pink. It's completely adorable.

"I didn't jump in front of the bullet," Hunter says,

but he takes Marv's hand anyway. "No need to thank me."

"You were there. If you weren't—" Marvin shakes his head "—she might not be here with us now. So, thank you."

I haven't thought a ton about that fact. I know Hunter saved my life by taking a bullet that most likely was meant for me. But I haven't thought about how truly close to death I came.

"You're welcome," Hunter says awkwardly, hating the attention but taking it all in stride.

Marvin doesn't waste any more time lingering because his beer is getting warm, and he has a few more to down before we close.

I don't know how the man is rail-thin. If I drank that many calories a day, I'd be as big as a balloon. My gut would be bloated, and none of my clothes would fit.

"Are you sure you're allowed to drink?" I ask Hunter, not yet knowing the details from his doctor's appointment.

"I'm allowed to do whatever I want, but I can't lift over forty pounds for the next few weeks."

"That's too bad," I tease him. "I was hoping you would give me a piggyback ride home."

"Baby, as soon as I can lift forty pounds, I'm tossing your ass over my shoulder and giving you an entirely different ride."

My mouth drops open. Who is this man, and where is the Hunter I knew? "Wow. Okay." I'd be lying if I said he doesn't make every little nerve ending in my body come alive.

He winces as he peers up at me, tearing at the label on his beer. "Too much?"

I shake my head. I clear my throat and pull at the collar of my sweater, suddenly overcome with heat. "No. It's perfect." My voice is huskier than normal, and I know he hears the tinge of need I don't bother to hide.

"Time's ticking," he says, glancing down at his watch. "Go finish up. I'll wait and plot."

Flashes of what the night is going to hold pop into my mind like a preview of a dirty movie. I stalk to the other end of the bar and fill a drink order before rounding into the general dining room. Before I go to the table, I stop by Hunter and lean over.

"I hope you're prepared," I whisper in his ear. "I'm going to rock your world tonight."

Hunter nearly knocks over his beer.

I walk away, leaving him damn near panting.

Checkmate.

CHAPTER 23
HUNTER

ZOEY'S KNEELING, staring up at me. "Are you sure about this?"

I touch her cheek, never more sure of anything in my life. "Are you?" Maybe she's having second thoughts but doesn't want to tell me.

She licks her lips, answering before she even has to say a word. "Yes." Her hands move to my jeans and start to work at undoing the button.

"We can wait," I offer, wanting to be certain she wants this. I know I'm overdoing it, but I don't want her to feel forced after everything she's been through.

"No," she says quickly and fingers the zipper, sliding it down as smoothly as possible in a pair this old. "I'm scared I'll hurt you. So, you've got to tell me if you need to stop."

"Sweetheart, touch my dick," I tell her, not wanting to have this conversation again.

I'm not breakable. If a bullet didn't take me out, having sex sure as hell won't.

We spent the last hour making out, and I was fine with that, but she wanted more. I let her take the lead, and that put us here.

Zoey smirks but doesn't hesitate to unzip my jeans and peel them away from my skin.

I unbutton my shirt but keep my eyes trained on her. She glances up as she slides her firm grip back and forth without pulling my dick out of my jeans. She's teasing me.

Carefully, I pull my arms out of my shirt and drop it to the floor next to her. Her hungry eyes travel up the length of me, soaking in every dip and ridge of the muscles on my chest and abdomen. Her eyes stop, studying, and I know where they are, staring at my incision and stitches.

"I'm fine," I tell her again, wanting to move forward instead of getting stuck in the past. "Don't stop that. It feels so good."

Her small hands move my jeans down my legs, and her gaze finally leaves my scar, going to my bare cock for the very first time.

"Well, I..." she mumbles, staring at it like a little kid at Christmas who got the most expensive present on their wish list. She licks her lips, and I nearly go weak in the knees. Between her hand wrapping around my shaft and the nearness of her mouth, I'm ready to beg for more.

When she leans forward and wraps her lips around the tip, I shiver. The feeling is better than I imagined. The warmth of her mouth against my needy skin has fireworks breaking out behind my eyelids as soon as they close.

She slides her hands from my hips to my ass and grips my cheeks roughly. Her tongue and mouth work my dick in perfect synchrony, sending shock waves throughout my entire system.

I don't know what I did to get so goddamn lucky to have found this woman and to have her want to be mine on top of it. But I'll be thanking my lucky stars for it until I draw my last breath.

It's been so long since I've been touched in this way that I have to concentrate hard not to tip over the edge too soon. I don't want this to be over before it's truly begun.

"Baby," I say softly, touching her hollowed-out cheek. "I need to taste you and be inside you."

Her gaze flicks up to me with my cock still deep in her mouth. She pulls back, letting me slide out of her lips in one fluid motion.

I almost whine at the loss of contact, but I keep my eyes on the prize, knowing the best is yet to come.

I hold out my hand as I kick my pants to the side, trying to avoid tripping and ruining the entire evening.

Zoey stands, and before I can reach out, she grabs the hem of the nightgown she put on after her shower and pulls it over her head.

My breath catches as I stare at her naked body. It's pure perfection and soft curves that are begging for my touch.

"Stunning," I whisper in the dim lighting of the room.

While she showered, I spent time adding a few candles around the room to create a soft glow because I needed to see every inch of her.

I reach out and grab her chin, tipping her head upward before taking her mouth in a deep kiss. I place my hand on her back, guiding us toward the bed behind her. When her knees touch the mattress, she sits down, but she never breaks the kiss.

"All the way," I tell her. "And spread your legs, sweetheart."

Without protest, she moves toward the head of the bed, all the while keeping eye contact with me. God, she's beautiful. When her head touches the pillow and her legs open, I slide my body over the bed until my face is right where it needs to be.

"Beautiful," I tell her, my warm breath skidding across her middle.

She moans as she tangles her fingers in my hair. "Sweetheart, lick my pussy," she says, throwing my earlier words back at me.

I can't wipe the stupid grin off my face as I lean forward, running my tongue over her sensitive skin. Her legs fall open even more as another moan slips out of her lips.

I don't go fast, feasting on her flesh in slow licks until my mouth latches on to the spot that I know will drive her wild. She bucks as soon as I suck, writhing underneath me as I try to hold her open with my arms wrapped around her thighs and my hands resting near her hips.

"Hunter," she calls out my name. I don't know if

she's begging for more or for me to slow down, but I keep up the pace, driving her closer to the edge. "I want you inside me."

We've already talked about this moment and the fact that she's on birth control. We've both been tested for every STI under the sun, and we're clean. There is no need for an extra barrier since she's been religious about taking her pill on time for years.

"Please," she begs.

I can't deny her anything, especially my dick.

I release my lips before climbing up her body, ignoring the pinch of pain from my wound.

I've lived through worse pain for very little payoff, but tonight, I'll let the pain mingle with the pleasure without a second thought.

"Condom?" I ask again, giving her the option in case she's changed her mind.

"No," she answers quickly, staring me straight in the eyes as I hover over her. "Are you okay?"

"Baby, I'm better than okay." I use one hand and line up my cock, letting the tip sink in slowly.

She winces at the first inch, and I take her lips with mine, swallowing down her moans and gasps. I move slowly, letting her get used to my size.

There's no feeling in the world that compares to being buried deep inside someone you care about. We've spent weeks building up to this moment, and it is worth every tease.

When my cock is buried to the hilt, I open my eyes and pull back. "You still okay?"

"Less talking and more fucking," she tells me before she pulls my face down toward hers. "Move."

I like a bossy woman, and an even bossier woman in bed is the sexiest thing in the world. I love never having to guess with her or wonder if she wants something. She's vocal and demanding. Two things I never thought I'd love, but hell, I do.

I move my hips slowly, thrusting in and out of her in no hurry. It is too damn good a feeling to move fast. I relish every tingle and shiver that course through my body at the contact.

Zoey's fingernails bite into the skin at my back, holding me to her as her feet dig into my ass. She pulls me toward her, wanting me to move faster and harder with each thrust.

I can't stop the orgasm that is about to crash over me. I can't slow it down. Not with the pace she's set. The way she moans my name and lets out little whimpers against my lips.

My lips crash into hers, sucking her moans into my mouth. Her body shakes underneath me before becoming rigid. Her pussy squeezes my cock, pulling me over the edge with her.

I moan through the pleasure and bite back a cry when my stitches pull at my skin. The mix of the two opposite sensations rocks my body with wave after wave of an orgasm that has me seeing stars behind my eyelids.

The only sounds in the room are our gasps for air afterward. I stare down at her as she stares up at me.

And all I see is my future.

EPILOGUE

ZOEY

THREE MONTHS LATER...

"Zoey, Zoey, Zoey," Amira says as she runs down the hallway toward me.

I brace myself, knowing the power of her hugs. Even though she's little, she packs one hell of a wallop when she comes at you at full force.

Hunter's a good twenty feet behind her, carrying two bags of groceries. "Amira," he calls out, but it's useless.

I open my arms as she springs into the air, colliding with me.

"Oof," I mutter, staggering backward, but I somehow find my footing and stay upright. I wrap my arms around her, giving her a giant bear hug. "What's up, sweetie?"

"Mom's better now," she says as she twirls a lock of my hair around her little finger.

"She is?" I knew her treatments had ended, and her newest scans came back showing no evidence of cancer.

She's currently in remission but will be monitored in case there's a reoccurrence.

"Yes." Amira's voice is so high-pitched it makes my ears ring. "Can we celebrate?"

"Of course." I kiss her cheeks, loving her excitement for all things. Her ability to celebrate every event in life is something I'll strive to do in the future myself. "What were you thinking?"

"We need a cake."

"Cupcakes?" I ask, preferring the frosting-to-cake ratio better than on a typical slice of cake.

"Even better." She turns to glance at her father without leaving my arms. "Daddy, can we make cupcakes?"

"Only if we can use sprinkles too," he tells her.

The man knows the way to a girl's heart. "Well, duh."

She says it so casually, I can't stop myself from laughing. This little girl has weaseled her way into my heart. At times, she's even made me question my decision to never have children of my own. My cousin and sister have done their best to make me believe that the pain is worth it, too. I still think they're lying, but if it happens in the future, I won't have a total meltdown.

I'm still on the pill. I haven't completely lost my marbles. We're nowhere near the kid talk. We've been dating for three months, and it's the longest I've ever been in a relationship with anyone in my life.

"Your place or mine?" I ask him when he gets close enough.

"Mine. Amira has all her things there."

It's a common question we seem to have every day. We stay in one person's place or the other's. At least it's easy since they're next to each other.

"You cook, I'll clean."

Hunter leans over and kisses my cheek, making Amira giggle. "Missed you," he whispers.

"Cupcakes," Amira calls out, wiggling out of my arms and interrupting the moment. She grabs my hand and then her father's, hauling us toward the door.

"Bossy little thing, aren't you?" I tease Amira, but my feet move because there's no point in fighting it.

"I'm making pasta. You hungry?" Hunter asks me.

"Starving." I haven't eaten all day. I had to go into the bar early this morning. It hadn't had a deep clean in weeks, and it needed it. I spent hours steam-mopping the floor and scouring every surface I could until the place was spotless.

"Get everything done?" he asks as he unlocks the door.

"Yep. Everything."

Hunter offered to come with me, but I wouldn't put him through that. I like things the way I like them, and I'm picky about the results.

"Hold this," Hunter says, placing something cool and hard in my hand.

I glance down, finding a new key. "What's this?" I ask as I follow him into his place.

"A key to my apartment. I thought you should have your own."

I gawk at him, my mind working faster than my mouth can catch up.

Amira kicks off her shoes and runs to her room, leaving us alone in the entryway.

"You're giving me a key."

"Is that okay?" he asks, setting the bags of groceries on the table near the door.

"Well, yeah, sure. I just wasn't expecting it."

I don't know why it feels like such a huge step. In the grand scheme of things, it's not. We've been playing apartment shuffle for months now. I don't know why I haven't given him a key to my place yet. I should've been the one to think of it first.

"No?" he asks.

I'm so busy staring at the key that I don't even notice when he drops down on one knee.

"What are you…" I don't get the sentence out before he reaches into his pocket and pulls out a small box.

My heart feels like it somersaults down from my chest and straight into my abdomen. Is he? Oh my God. He's… Fuck. We've talked about the future and what that would look like for us. Of course, we've talked about getting married and our forever, but I didn't think it would come this soon.

"Zoey Gallo, will you do me the honor of marrying me? It doesn't have to be soon, but I can't go another day without having you as my fiancée. I want forever. There's not a day I want to draw breath where you aren't mine. Now and always." He holds out the box and flips open the top.

My breath catches when the overhead lights glint off the ring. It's stunning. Not overly large, but I'm not into jewelry. It's the perfect size and shape—princess cut.

My vision becomes blurry as I try to gaze down at him. My lips quiver as I try to speak. I give up, holding out my hand in front of me. "Yes," I cry, nearly dropping to my knees in front of him.

How could I not say yes? The man took a bullet for me, and not a day has gone by since he entered my life that I haven't felt safe and loved.

He's everything I wanted but didn't think was ever possible. I've spent most of my life with the wrong type, always bumping into the assholes who only wanted me for one thing. But every single horrible encounter was worth it because now I have Hunter.

When he slides the ring on my finger, I throw myself into his arms, and he falls backward onto his ass. I pepper his face with kisses before I finally find his mouth, kissing him with all the emotion I feel in this moment.

Is this quick? Hell yeah, it is. Am I good with it? Hell yeah, I am. I've been with enough bad to know when something special lands in my lap, and I'll do anything to hold on to him, including becoming his wife.

Hunter holds me tight as I deepen the kiss.

Amira gasps, and I pull back like we've been caught by our parents.

"Did you ask her, Daddy?"

He blows out a breath and climbs to his feet, somehow holding on to me while he does it. The man is strong, and I freaking love that for me. "I did, sweetheart. She said yes."

"You knew?" I ask Amira.

My parents never would've trusted me with a secret so big at her age. Even now, I'm not sure they would, but that goes for everyone in the family.

She nods, practically squealing. "I did." She runs toward us, colliding with her father's side and wrapping her arms around his legs. "She's going to marry us."

I chuckle, loving how she's included herself. And she isn't wrong.

They're a package deal, and now I'm part of it too.

"Cupcakes," Amira says, reminding us of our earlier promise.

"I'll help her with them while you make dinner," I tell Hunter as my feet finally touch the floor.

He lifts my hand, kissing my finger where the ring meets my skin. "I like this."

"Me too," I tell him, and I mean all of it.

The ring.

The kid.

Us.

Our future.

The happily ever after I always wanted but never thought I'd get.

The wish that finally came true.

Ready for more Sinners?
Mason Gallo's story is next!
>> Tap here to grab your copy *of Desire*

NEED MORE MEN OF INKED CHICAGO?

Join the Chicago Gallo Family with their strong alphas, sassy women, and tons of fun.

Book 1 - Maneuver (Lucio)
Book 2 - Flow (Daphne)
Book 3 - Hook (Angelo)
Book 4 - Hustle (Vinnie)
Book 5 - Love (Angelo)

Men of Inked Southside Boxset

The Men of Inked Southside series is also available in discreet paperback format for your enjoyment…

♥ Men of Inked Reader Guide ♥

DOWNLOAD NOW

Tap here to get the Men of Inked Reader Guide,
which includes a family tree, printable reading guide, and
information about each Gallo family saga read.

MEN OF *inked* MYSTERY BOX

DELIVERED EVERY THREE MONTHS

SPECIAL EDITION HARDCOVER & EXCLUSIVE MERCHANDISE!

CHELLEBLISSROMANCE.COM

START AT THE VERY BEGINNING...

THROTTLE ME - MEN OF INKED
BOOK 1

Suzy

The moonlight filtered through the pine trees lining the fields, leaving shadows on the pavement. The crisp air that had been missing for months caressed my skin. I couldn't wait to crawl in my bed and close my eyes, getting lost in a dream world that had nothing to do with my current reality.

The night had been perfect. I'd had dinner and drinks with my best friend, Sophia, and although I was exhausted from a long workday, I felt a sense of serenity. Spending time with Sophia always made me happy. She was like a sister to me, especially when she had lived with me for over a year. I felt like part of me had been missing since the day she moved out, leaving me behind.

Dancing in the seat, screaming out the lyrics, I thought about how I wanted someone that would do everything the song described. No one had ever made me feel that way. The steering wheel shook in my hands and a screeching sound pulled me out of my trance.

"Damn it," I said, hitting the steering wheel with my palm.

The orange flash from my hazards blinked against the dark pavement as I pulled off the road and my car sputtered to a stop. Bad luck seemed to follow me. I squeezed the steering wheel, trying to calm my frazzled nerves. I knew the day would come, the day my car would die, but I prayed it would happen after my next paycheck…no such luck.

Resting my head on the wheel, I closed my eyes, taking a deep breath. "Great, just freaking great." I rocked back and forth, feeling sorry for myself, hitting my head on the cool plastic. I thought about whom to call or where to walk. I hadn't passed a gas station or even a damn streetlight in miles. Without picking up my head, I reached for my phone, bringing it to my eyes.

"Shit." The screen wouldn't power on after I hit every button I could think to press. It was useless. It was dead and now I was totally stranded. What else could possibly go wrong? Sighing, I sat up and glanced in the rearview mirror, but only the shadows from the trees filled my view. No cars, neon signs, or streetlights. Shit.

I placed my hand on my chest to feel the beat of my heart, which was so hard I swear it was audible. Visions from slasher movies flooded my mind. Girl deserted on the side of the road until she's found by a handsome stranger that ends up being a serial killer.

Should I start walking to God knows where? Do I just sit there and wait for a stranger to offer me help? I never liked feeling helpless—I was too smart to be helpless, but it was the only thing I felt in this moment. It could be hours before someone found me in my car.

I grabbed my purse, dead phone, and keys, and climbed out of the car. My feet ached in the extra-high heels I wore. Leaning against the car, I gave my feet a moment to adjust, as I looked in both directions. Neither of my options were good and I was exhausted. My feet screamed from standing still. Thank God I could sleep in tomorrow after the way this evening was ending. There was a gas station a couple miles back—better to go with what I knew than to walk into an uncertain future. I tapped the lock button on my key chain one more time, helping relieve my OCD need to double-check everything, before I started walking away.

Barely clearing the trunk, a single light came over a small hill in the distance, hurting my eyes with the brightness. The roar of the engine grew louder as the distance closed. I waved my arms as a figure came into view, but the asshole biker drove right passed me as I screamed, "Hey! Hey!" The wind from his bike caused the dust on the road to kick up and fill my mouth.

I turned around, coughing, and screamed toward the bike. I knew it was pointless. There was no way in hell he'd heard me yelling above the roar of his bike, but he had to see me. The red taillight lit up the road as he turned the bike in my direction. I swallowed hard, unsure if this was my best idea of the night—but I'd already made too many mistakes to dwell on that. He was my only hope of getting home.

I stood there like a deer in headlights, unable to move, as I gaped at him. My hands trembled as the figure on the bike came to a stop. The engine was almost deafening, as I took in the sight of him on the machine. The bike was a Harley, a Fat Boy, with no windshield, chrome handlebars, and a dark body. He wore black boots, dark jeans, and a dark t-shirt. He was large and muscular, and I sucked in a breath as my eyes reached his handsome and rugged face. A playful grin danced on his lips as he watched me ogle him.

Shit.

"Need some help?" he asked, removing his helmet, running his fingers through his disheveled hair. The dark peaks stood up on the top, the sides were short and clipped, and the color matched the sky—dark. I couldn't see his eyes; a pair of tinted glasses hid them. Could serial killers be so sexy?

"Um, do you have a cell phone I could use to call for a ride?" I asked without taking a step in his direction. *Don't get too close—leave room to run.* Who the hell was I kidding? I couldn't make it five feet in these damn shoes.

"Sure." As he leaned back on his bike, I studied his body as he dug in his pocket. The skintight jeans showed his muscles through the denim fabric. Everything clung to him. I wanted to poke him to see if he felt as hard as he looked. What was wrong with me?

I was too busy staring to notice what he was holding out for me. "Lady, you wanted my phone?"

Snapping back to reality with the sound of his deep voice, I took a step toward him, reaching for the phone. "Oh, sorry."

My fingertips grazed his palm, and a tiny shock passed between us. His fingers closed on my hand as I pulled away. My heartbeat, which had calmed, now began to pound feverishly in my chest. It had to be my hormones. I hadn't had sex in God knows how long—I stopped counting after three months. The man in front of me wasn't my type, but his sex appeal wasn't lost on me. He looked like a whole lot of trouble, and I didn't need that in my life.

I stepped back, keeping my eyes trained on him, as I dialed the only person close enough to help—Sophia. The phone rang and his eyes traveled up and down the length of my body—with each ring, my stomach began to turn. I didn't have anyone else to call.

Tapping the end button, I sighed. "There's no answer. Thanks." I gave him a sheepish smile as I handed him the phone.

"Let me take a look and see if there's anything I can do. Okay?" he asked, as he began angling the bike to shine the headlights on the hood.

"Sure." I hit the unlock button on my car key before climbing in. I put the key in the ignition, but stayed aware of his proximity. No one would hear me scream if he tried to kill me. I couldn't let my guard down.

He put the kickstand down, climbed off the bike, and placed the helmet on the seat. Pulling the hood latch next to my seat, I watched him from the relative darkness of my car, my face hidden by shadows. He was large, larger than he looked sitting on the Harley. He had to be more than a foot taller than me, and looked more solid with the bike illuminating his body. I stared at him, mouth open slightly, my breathing shallow as I looked at him like a piece of meat through the gap between the hood. He oozed masculinity and ruggedness, and I tried to picture him without all the skintight clothes. The muscles in his arm rippled as he touched the parts under the hood.

What would it be like to be with a man like him? Every man I'd dated just didn't work out. They were nice guys, but the spark I wanted was always missing. People think I'm a good girl, and I am, but my mind is filled with dirty thoughts that I could never share with a mate. I'd shared them with Sophia, but she doesn't count. No one had ever done anything fantasy-worthy with me. I can barely speak the words that are needed to describe the things I want done to me, or that I'd want to do to another person in this world.

"Ma'am," he said, snapping me out of the evaluation of my sex life, or lack thereof.

"Sorry, yes?"

"Can you try and start it for me, please?" he said, leaning over the hood, his hands placed on either side of the opening. "Now," he said. The car churned and churned. "Stop," I heard him yell over the screeching noise. He moved methodically around the engine. "Try it again." I turned the key, causing the engine to rattle, but not start.

He stood, rubbing the back of his neck as curses spilled from his lips. The only thing I could see was his crotch. I stared, motionless. His t-shirt covered the belt loops and stopped just above his groin. Damn. He filled out those jeans. He had to be big. Everything about him was big—he couldn't, just couldn't, have a small cock, could he?

The last guy that I'd slept with was more the size of a party pickle. It was the most unsatisfying sexual experience of my life. He was a teacher, and I wanted someone who was educated and self-sufficient, but he was boring in and out of the bedroom. I thought I'd found that with Derek, Mr. Pickle, but I was wrong. He was a wreck, and filled with more mental issues than anyone I'd ever know. He was germophobic, which was problematic when having sex. He'd jump right out of bed immediately after sex to shower and wash the dirty off. I sighed to myself, remembering his need to be clean—never mind that he was an asshole, too.

The hood of my car made a loud thump as the man slammed it. "Your car is a little tricky. Foreign cars can be complicated. I can't seem to get it to start," he said, walking toward the driver-side door.

"It's okay. Thanks for trying." I climbed out, not wanting to be trapped inside. What the hell was I going to do now?

"I was heading to the bar up the road. Want to join me?" He smiled and tilted his head as he studied me. "You can call a tow truck from there. It may take a while for them to get out here."

I couldn't think of any other option. He was my only hope, my saving grace from the dark roadside, and a means to an end. There were worse things than climbing on the back of his motorcycle and wrapping my arms around him. "Okay, but I've never been on a bike."

"Never? How is that even possible?" he asked, shaking his head, a small laugh escaping his lips. His teeth sparkled in the light, straight and white. His jaw was strong, his cheekbones jutted out more when he smiled, and a small dimple formed on the left side of his face.

I looked down at the ground, my cheeks heated. "I don't know. I just never knew anyone that had one and I find them totally scary."

"It's not far from here and there isn't much traffic. I'll keep you safe," he said, holding out his helmet.

My stomach fluttered as I closed the car door and thought about my first motorcycle ride. The black, round helmet felt cool against my fingers as I took it from him. I scrunched my eyebrows together as I studied it. I didn't know if there was a front or a back, or how to put it on.

"Here, let me help you," he said as he reached for the helmet, removing it from my grip. His hand touched mine and I felt the spark again. Not a real spark, but electricity that I felt with every fiber of my being from the slightest touch. My body wanted his touch, but my mind was throwing up the caution flag.

Placing it gently on my head, he ran his rough fingers down the straps, almost caressing my skin, to adjust it to fit my face. I inhaled deeply, trying to fill all my senses with him. He smelled different than any other man I'd smelled. He didn't smell of cheap cologne, but there was a spicy, woodsy scent that reminded me of home. I closed my eyes and relished the feel of his warm skin against mine.

"All done. Are you ready?" he asked.

I opened my eyes, heat creeping up my neck, as I had been lost in his touch. "Yes." I prayed my voice didn't betray me.

He climbed on the bike, sliding forward, making room for me. "Lift your leg and climb on."

Placing my hand on his shoulder to help balance myself, I followed his instructions; my body slid forward, smashing against him. Rock solid. He turned his head, looking me in the eyes. "Put your feet on the pegs and wrap your arms around me. I don't bite—well, unless you want me to." He smirked, and my heart felt like it was doing the tango in my chest as I pressed against his back. He didn't just say that to me, did he? I lifted my feet off the ground, turning over complete control to the stranger I was entrusting with my life. I locked my hands together, completely wrapped around him.

"Ready?"

"Wait! I don't even know your name. I mean, I'm putting my life in your hands and I don't even know who you are." I gripped his body tighter, clinging to him.

I couldn't hear his laughter, but I felt the rumble of it from deep in his chest. "My friends call me City, sugar." He throttled the engine and my heart skipped a beat. Fear gripped me—there was no turning back now.

My grip became viselike, fear overcoming any need

to be cool or seem calm in front of him. He patted my hands before the bike began to move, and I couldn't bear to look. I buried my face in his back, avoiding any chance of seeing the road. The wind caressed my skin, causing it to feel like ice compared to the warmth my palms experienced. Did this man have any soft spots? I flexed my fingers against his chest, wanting to feel his hardness, praying like hell I made it seem natural and not like I was molesting him.

The bike picked up speed, and my heart thundered against his back. I gripped him harder, holding on for dear life, the sound of the engine drowning out everything else around me, except the two of us. He leaned into the bike, his ass moving snugly between my legs. I didn't dare move. He was warm, comfortable, and I enjoyed every minute my body touched his. I closed my eyes, trying to not think about the movement of the bike underneath us—the slight shift and unevenness of the road made me feel off balance.

The noise of the engine changed, and I finally peeked over his shoulder. The parking lot of the Neon Cowboy was packed with bikes and was the brightest thing for miles. I'd driven by it dozens of times, but never thought about stopping. This wasn't the type of bar for kids on speedy, foreign-made bikes, but a place for tough bikers to hang out, drink beer, and pick up chicks.

City backed the bike into an empty spot, and I could feel my body begin to tremble from the fear that finally began to seep through my veins. I did it. I rode on a motorcycle, and with a stranger, no less. My breath was harsh as I blinked slowly and tried to calm myself down.

"You can climb off now, sugar." His legs were straddling the bike and he held the handlebars, securing the bike for me. "Enjoy your first ride?"

I released my hands from the security of his body and hoisted myself off on trembling legs. "It was the single most terrifying thing I've ever experienced," I said, thankful when my feet were firmly on the ground. I stood, trying to get my body to stop shaking and my heart to slow down before walking inside the bar with him at my side.

"If that's the scariest thing you've ever experienced, you need to get out more, sugar. I took it slow with you." He grinned, and my stomach plummeted from his sinful smile. I wanted to see him above me naked and moving in and out of my body slowly, almost at a torturous pace. Everything about him made my body convulse and scream for attention. He wasn't my type. I preferred a bookworm and a man that liked to spend an evening inside watching a movie or playing Scrabble, not riding like a bat out of hell on a Fat Boy to hang out at a bar. I wasn't a barfly and never would be.

The outdoor lights gave me a full view of the man that called himself City. His hair was darker than I originally thought, almost jet black, and an inch long on the top, brushing against his forehead as he shook it out. It was a mess from the wind, with the front hanging over his forehead. I couldn't tell the color of his eyes; they were still hidden behind the tinted lenses of his glasses.

"Yeah, lucky me." I chuckled and tried to play it

cool, even though my body shook. If that was slow, I didn't think I wanted to know what his idea of fast and hard were—or did I? Damn. He had my brain all jumbled.

After removing the helmet, I ran my fingers through my hair, trying to straighten it after the wild ride. He laughed as he crawled off the bike, taking the helmet from my hands, and placed it on the seat. I watched, mesmerized, as he removed his glasses and put them inside a small bag hanging from the side of the bike. I wanted to see his eyes, and the entire man without a mask or veil.

"Ready, babe?" He motioned toward the door.

I wanted to scream no, but I didn't have a choice. I could never walk into this sort of place on my own.

"Yeah, ready as I'll ever be." I started walking toward the door and felt a hand on my arm, stopping me in my tracks. I looked at his fingers wrapped around my arm and turned toward him. "What are you doing?"

"You can't just walk into a place like this. You're an outsider. They'll eat you alive in there. I don't want anyone giving you shit. We have to make them believe you're with me so they leave you alone. Unless you want the attention?" he asked with a crooked eyebrow.

"I don't." I didn't mind the idea of making everyone in the bar think we were together. City was hot and seemed like a nice guy; he did stop to help me when he could've driven right by me.

"Just stay by my side and follow my lead. I know these people and I don't want them sniffing around you. They look for easy prey," he said, giving me a smile that made my body tingle and my sex convulse.

"Okay, I'll stick to you like glue and follow your lead." Jesus, I sounded like a dork. I've always been a bookworm. I was national honor society member, and when all my friends were partying, I stayed in my dorm to study.

City nestled me against his side, tucking me between his body and arm. I moved with him, trying to keep up with his fluid movements, but my legs were so short I felt like I almost had to jog to keep time with him. He opened the door and I was immediately hit with a smoky smell, loud, twangy music, and a dozen set of eyes looking directly at us.

Randomly people yelled out "City" throughout the bar, giving me a clue that he was a regular. I felt like I'd entered a seedy version of *Cheers* and City was Norm, only sexy and muscular. He leaned down, placing his mouth next to my ear. I felt his hot breath before I could hear his words.

"Stick close and show no fear," he whispered, causing goose bumps to break out across my skin. "Let's say hello then we'll call a tow for you."

City looked big enough to handle any man in this place, but I didn't want to take that chance. I concentrated on breathing, keeping my chin up, and watching where I walked. The floor was filled with peanut shells and dust, and it made the walk in the stilettos even more treacherous than normal. I could barely walk when I bought them, but they looked too sexy to pass up.

We walked to a table filled with men all wearing their leather vests, covered in patches. They were unshaven, as dangerously sexy as City, with mischievous smiles on their faces. "Who's this lovely lady, City?" one man asked. His eyes raked up my body, stopping at my breasts before he looked at my face.

"This is Sunshine. Don't even think about it, Tank, she's with me," City said with a smile on his face as he pulled me closer.

Sunshine? I'd never told him my name and he never asked. I didn't like the way Tank looked at me. Thank God he wasn't the one driving by while I was stranded. He looked at me like I was a piece of meat, a meal for his enjoyment.

Tank put his hands up in surrender. "Dude, I'd never. Chill out. I'm just enjoying the view," he said, his eyes moving from City to me, and not being coy about his visual molestation.

City squeezed my waist. "Sunshine, this is Tank, the asshole. This is Hog, Frisco, and Bear," he said, pointing to each of the men.

The nicknames didn't seem to fit any of the men, except Bear. His arms were hairy and he was big, huge, in fact, with dark hair and a fuzzy face. He looked huggable and kind, with soft hazel eyes.

"Hi," I said, looking at each of them quickly, but I didn't try to memorize their names.

"I didn't know you were bringing a woman tonight, City," Bear said.

"Wilder shit *has* happened, Bear," City said, pulling me closer, leaving no space between us.

"She doesn't look like your usual taste, my friend." Bear smirked. "I don't mean that shitty, girl, I just mean you're one fine piece of ass and too good for that low-life motherfucker. You should be sitting on my lap." He patted his leg, and I wanted to find an exit. I looked down and studied my clothes. I didn't wear the trashy clothes some of the women in here wore, but I looked classy, sexy even, with not a hint of nerd to be found.

City moved toward Bear, and my heart sank as he began to speak. "Show some respect, you asshole. That's not how you talk to a lady." City stood inches from Bear's face. "Apologize to the lady. *Now*." City towered over him as Bear stayed rooted in his chair.

Bear looked at me, and I could see him swallow hard before he spoke. "I'm sorry, Sunshine. I was just kidding around. I really am an asshole. Forgive me, please."

"No harm done, Bear," I said with a fake smile, hoping to calm the situation.

"We're going to sit at the bar." City looked at Bear, not moving his eyes.

"Come on, dude, sit with us. Don't mind Bear. He's a total dick. Make his ass go sit at the bar," Frisco said.

"Sunshine and I want to be alone. I'll catch you guys another night," City said, pressing his hand against my back, guiding me away from the table and the large bar area.

"I'm sorry. They can be childish dicks. Bear doesn't have a filter," he said as he pulled out a chair for me. City had manners. Not many of the men I dated did something as simple as pull out a chair for a lady—it was a lost art. "He's a good guy, but sometimes his mouth runs and he doesn't think before he speaks."

"It's okay, really...it is. Thanks for sticking up for me," I said to him as I sat down, pulling my stool closer to the bar. "Why did you call me Sunshine?"

"Well, I don't know your name and you remind me of sunshine—your hair is golden and your smile glows. Just sounded right. I had to come up with something on the fly," he said. "I hope you didn't mind." He shrugged and grabbed the menu lying nearby.

"I didn't mind, but my name is Suzy."

"What would you like, Suzy?"

I wanted to say "you," because somehow this man made me lose my grip on reality. "Virgin daiquiri, please."

"Virgin? Really?" His brows shot up and the corner of his mouth twitched.

"I already had a drink tonight. I just want something sweet, no liquor."

"Do you want something to eat?" he asked. "You a vegetarian too?" He laughed.

"Shut up." I smacked him on the arm. "I'm good. I just want to call a tow truck."

"Gotcha." He pulled out his phone and placed it on the bar. "Hey, darlin', can you put in an order for a cheeseburger, a beer, and a virgin daiquiri?" he asked the bartender.

"Sure thing, handsome," she said, walking away, slowly swaying her hips to grab attention. I turned to City to see if he was watching her, but he was staring at me instead, and my mouth felt dry and scratchy.

"You want to call Triple A or someone else?" he asked without taking his eyes off me. They were an amazing shade of blue, and I couldn't look away. I'd always loved my blue eyes, but his were almost turquoise. I felt like he was staring through me, into me, seeing everything I hid under the surface. I wanted him, but I didn't want to admit my attraction. I *couldn't* admit it.

"Triple A is good," I said, reaching for my purse to find my membership card. I fumbled with my wallet, finding the card behind everything else inside. I could feel his eyes on me; he studied me and it made me nervous. What was he thinking? I dialed the number as I swiveled away from him, needing to avert his stare.

"Hello, Triple A, how can I help you?"

I could barely hear the tiny female voice above the loud classic rock that pulsed throughout the smoky bar. City chatted with the bartender as I tried to drown them out and give my location and details about my car. They wouldn't be able to make it out to my car until morning. I thanked her for helping me before hitting the end button.

"What'd they say?" City asked with a sincere look as the bartender sashayed away from us.

"They won't make it out here until morning because they're busy and we're in the middle of nowhere. I'm to leave it unlocked so they can get in and put it in neutral or something. I don't know how it works. I've never had my car towed before." Now what the hell was I going to do? I was stranded at the Neon Cowboy with Mr. Sexalicious and my dirty thoughts.

"I'll bring you back to your car when I'm done eating. I guess you'll need a lift home too?" he asked, sipping his drink as he eyed me.

I smiled at him. Though I hated the thought of him going out of his way, and I wasn't that comfortable with a stranger knowing where I lived, I couldn't say no. "I'd appreciate it, if you don't mind."

"Not at all, Suzy. I can't just leave you here and walk out the door. I got ya, babe." He turned his stool toward me and leaned into my space. "Where do you want me to take you after we leave? Home?" He quirked an eyebrow, waiting for my response, and held me in place with his hard stare.

Home? Whose home was he referring to? City looked to be the type that had different women falling out of his bed every morning...or maybe he kicked them out before he fell asleep. His fingers brushed against the top of my hand and my internal dialogue evaporated.

"Where. Do. You. Live?" The laughter he tried to hide behind his hand made it clear that I'd sat there longer in thought than I had realized.

I cleared my throat. "I need to unlock my car then I need a lift home. I live about fifteen minutes north. Is that okay? I mean, I don't want to—" He put his finger over my lips and stopped me mid-sentence.

"Doesn't matter, I'll take you anywhere," he said with a sly grin that made my pulse race and my body heat. He licked his lips, and I stared like an idiot. My sex convulsed at the thought of his lips on my skin. What the hell was wrong with me? Every movement he made and word he spoke turned sexual, as if permeating my brain. I needed to get laid; this man was not hitting on me, was he?

"You want some? I can't eat it all," he said as the plate was placed in front of him.

I shook my head and picked up my drink, trying to cool my body off from the internal fire caused by City. The cool, sweet strawberry slush danced across my tongue and slid down my throat.

I swirled the red straw in my mouth, trying to occupy my mind. His arms flexed as he lifted the burger to his mouth, forearms covered with tattoos. The left arm had various designs woven together—a koi fish, a tiger, and a couple of other nature-themed pieces that seemed to move across his skin, and his right arm had a city skyline. I wanted to touch his arms and run my fingers across his ink. He looked big everywhere, and my gaze drifted down his body and lingered at his crotch. I wondered if his motorcycle and tattoos made up for shortcomings elsewhere, but I couldn't believe a man like him was tiny. There was no way in hell he had a party...

"Pickle?"

I blinked and moved my eyes away from his crotch to his eyes. *Pickle?* He held it and motioned for me to take it.

"No. Thanks, though. You eat it," I said, feeling like he was reading my mind. God, I hoped he didn't see me staring at his crotch. I sucked down the rest of my drink, wishing now that it did have alcohol in it. Maybe then I wouldn't feel so embarrassed. "I noticed your tattoos. What's the one on your right arm?"

"That's the Chicago skyline," he said, as he took another bite.

"You from there?"

"Born and bred, baby." He grunted and continued to chew. I couldn't take my eyes off his mouth. Watching him eat was erotic to me; his lips moved as he chewed, and he sucked each finger in his mouth to clean off the juices that flowed from the sandwich. Damn. It *had* been too long since I'd had sex—when eating becomes sexual. Houston, we have a problem.

Ready to start at the very beginning with the Gallo family?
Download THROTTLE ME and join the sexy fun!

To purchase signed paperbacks and more, please visit
chelleblissromance.com

ABOUT THE AUTHOR

I'm a full-time writer, time-waster extraordinaire, social media addict, coffee fiend, and ex-history teacher. *To learn more about my books, please visit menofinked.com.*

Want to stay up-to-date on the newest Men of Inked release and more? Tap here to join my newsletter or visit *menofinked.com/inked-news*

Join over 10,000 readers on Facebook in Chelle Bliss Books private reader group and talk books and all things reading. Tap here to become part of the family or visit at *facebook.com/groups/blisshangout*

Tap here to see the Gallo Family Tree or visit *menofinked.com/gallo-family-tree*

Where to Follow Me:

facebook.com/authorchellebliss1

instagram.com/authorchellebliss

bookbub.com/authors/chelle-bliss

goodreads.com/chellebliss

amazon.com/author/chellebliss

tiktok.com/@chelleblissauthor

pinterest.com/chellebliss10

www.ingramcontent.com/pod-product-compliance
Lightning Source LLC
Chambersburg PA
CBHW011119100726

47898CB00011B/3150

www.ingramcontent.com/pod-product-compliance
Lightning Source LLC
Chambersburg PA
CBHW011118100726
47898CB00011B/3141